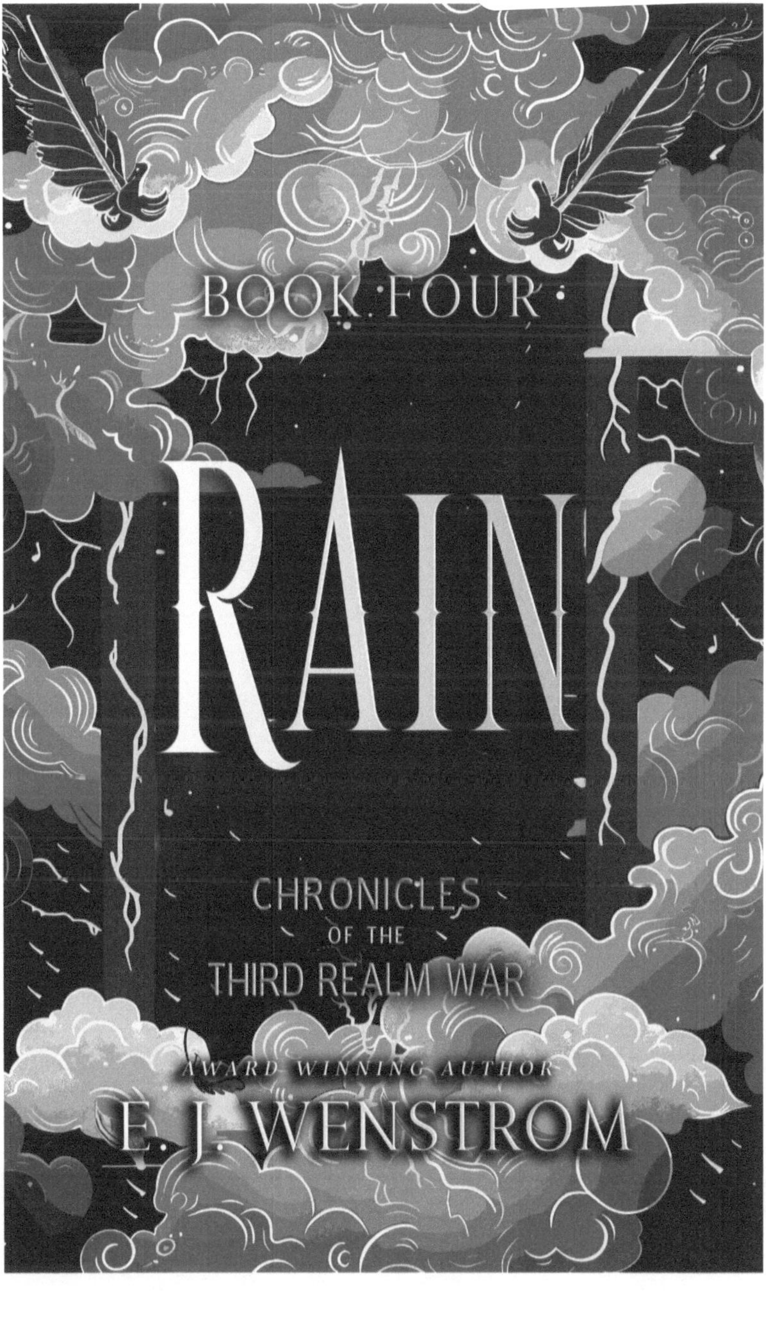

BOOK FOUR

RAIN

CHRONICLES
OF THE
THIRD REALM WAR

AWARD-WINNING AUTHOR
E. J. WENSTROM

First published by City Owl Press.

Praise for the Chronicles of the Third Realm War Series

"Combining the lush charms of fantasy with the highs and lows of a tragic love story."

— *READERS LANE*

"A gritty story that holds within it, a raw romance—Rain delivers."

—*Southern Gothic and Magical Realism Author, Em Shotwell*

"[Rain] was haunting, heartbreaking, and did not turn out the way I expected it to."

—*Amazon Review*

"After a delightful series of riveting twists and turns, Wenstrom delivered something both unexpected and inevitable."

— *Nicholas Lemieux Reviews*

"From beginning to end, a thoroughly enjoyable story that any lover of fantasy stories will be able to lose themselves in."

— *In D'Tale Magazine*

"In the Third Realm, perils await, but anything is possible—and readers who venture there will find a rewarding escape into a very creative and fully imagined world."

— *Literary Hill*

"Mimicking the brutal and the strange of ancient mythology alongside the high fantasy and gut wrenching action of desperate warfare, Wenstrom does it again."

—Readers Lane

"With each book, Wenstrom gives us more and more depth to her world and characters."

—Amazon reader review

Continue the Third Realm War series

The realm is falling apart.
The demigods are breaking free.
The gods are nowhere to be found.

There is only one escape from Adem's curse: A soul of his own.

Read the full series on Kindle Unlimited
All formats at EJWenstrom.com

The realm is falling apart.
The demigods are breaking free.
The gods are nowhere to be found.

Rona didn't ask to be brought back from the dead. Now that she's back, she's angry enough to raise hell.

Read the full series on Kindle Unlimited
All formats at EJWenstrom.com

The realm is falling apart.
The demigods are breaking free.
The gods are nowhere to be found.

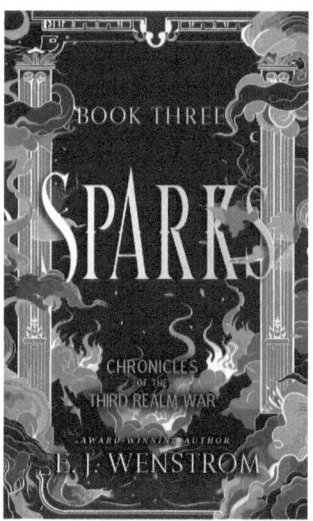

Being Chosen by the Gods doesn't mean much when they have abandoned you.

Join E. J. Wenstrom's Monstrosity

Stay in touch with the weekly newsletter

JOIN E. J.'s MONSTROSITY newsletter for sci-fi and fantasy, publishing and other news highlights weekly, plus download the Third Realm War prequel novella.

Subscribe now at EJWenstrom.com

For Pippi, who cuddled up with me every day while I wrote this, kept the barking to a minimum, and sometimes hogged the blanket.
And for Christopher, always.

Contents

CHAPTER ONE

IT HAPPENED BEFORE I could stop myself—my hand reached out and stroked the angel Calipher's wing. It seemed perfectly harmless.

As my fingers reached into the soft feathers, a surge of peace broke through me like an unexpected breeze. When I pulled away, the vacuum it left behind flooded with shame. I realized, too late, I'd stolen something I had no right to.

Now, Calipher turns around, searching.

"Who did it?" he demands. His wings, like great founts of silver sprouting from his shoulders, bristle. "Who touched my wing?"

My heart pounds and my chest floods with panic. I want to run and hide, but my feet are planted to the ground as if roots have sprouted from them and bind me here.

What is wrong with me? I should never have touched him. But his aura gives off what I crave most—more today than ever. Deep peace pours out of him, like the quiet trickle of a forest creek.

Heat rushes to my face, and I am sure a deep flush will give me away.

"Who touched my wing?" Calipher repeats.

Tousled golden locks fall onto his face. The feathers of his wings quiver and pull away from his back. He is glorious and beautiful and terrible. For the first time in all the years since the goddess Theia sent him to us, I am afraid of him.

I have always been jealous of the way he could fly away into the skies any time the realm of Terath might become too much for him. Sometimes, his wings seem like the most magnificent things that could ever be, the way they spread around him, bright and gleaming. *He* seems like the most magnificent thing that could ever be. Sometimes, I want that magnificence for myself.

Calipher's great shadow casts about as he turns to look for the culprit. He is larger than any human, perfectly lean and tall. His skin glows pale as the moon, and his great silvery wings spread wide, the tips catching the morning sun with an orange glint, like embers at the edge of a fire. He is wild and alive, and he has never looked more enthralling.

It makes me want to touch him all over again.

The busy morning villagers—Shara, who I just traded with, Cyril, our closest neighbor and fellow farmer, all of them—step away, creating a halo of space between him and the crowd. As always, they are afraid of him. Afraid of his large-ness. Afraid of his magic. Of his wings and his glow and all that makes him beautiful. They are afraid of his other-ness, and all it implies.

"Come forth," Calipher urges. "Who was it?"

The others back away more, murmuring among themselves in fear. I'm the only one who doesn't, transfixed by his ire.

He turns slowly, looking over the gathering crowd. He looks right past me into the mass of faces.

He is so close, close enough to reach out and touch again, and yet still he barely even sees me. I can't bear it anymore.

"It was me." The words crash out of me and shatter like clay pots.

In their wake, the most painful kind of silence falls over the village center. Calipher stops his pacing. He stares at me. They all do.

My face burns with shame and I can't bear to hold his gaze. What is wrong with me? Why, this day of all days, could I no longer hold myself back?

After all these years, with day after day of pain piling onto my soul, I could not stand to *not* touch him any longer.

I woke up this morning to find Mother had disappeared again.

Mother does not disappear in the typical way, where a person cannot be found. For her, it is more as though she drowns inside herself, and her body becomes an empty shell. Even after all these years, my father's death still festers in her like an infected wound. It is as if she spends her life treading water, fighting to keep herself at the surface. And then sometimes she gets too tired, and the pain overcomes her, and she slips under the surface, drowning.

When she drowns, she fumbles through her days barely seeing the next step in front of her, blindly stumbling through her routine in nothingness, unable to see even me.

There is nothing to be done about it. It simply is, like the tides. But I feel my father's absence, too. It burns at me like coals trapped in a furnace. When she drowns, the silence she leaves behind burns inside me, each time a little deeper into my soul.

The release of touching Calipher's wing was one I needed desperately.

And now?

I do not know what now. But I cannot bear to be here anymore, facing the bewilderment that wrinkles Calipher's brow.

I turn and shove my way through the collecting crowd. It is too much, and I have to get away, a stinging shame coursing through me.

Could I have held back, if I had known the chaos my small moment of indulgence would lead to? If I am honest with myself, I am not sure. Even with the harsh glares and mystified glances the townspeople give me as I shove past them, that small moment when his peace rushed over me—it was just what my soul needed.

My feet propel me away from Calipher, away from the village, into the forgiving cover of the forest. Only when I am enclosed in its depths do I stop and catch my breath.

As my breathing steadies and I slow to a walk, a shadow rushes around me, then pulls together into a figure at my side.

"Not now, Bastus."

I glance at him. His icy blue eyes are completely blank—the only thing that gives him away as a demon, rather than a human—but the rest of his face is solemn.

"Nia," he greets me. He studies my face and tilts his head. "What troubles you? Is Lina at it again?"

Bastus knows more than most what my mother is. He was there when my father died years ago, and he watched with me in the weeks after as something in her died in her, too.

"Yes," I reply. "But this isn't about Mother."

Standing so close, I can feel his aura vibrating off of his skin. He's a creature of Shael, god of chaos. While Calipher's aura is so soothing, Bastus' strains me with restlessness.

"What is it, then?"

He means to help, but his aura goes where he goes, like a shadow. It is like a poker shaking up embers from the coals, waking up the things inside me that I try to suppress.

"It's nothing." I sigh.

I lie to him reflexively, even though I know he won't believe me.

He folds his arms over his chest, accentuating his strong, square shoulders, and waits. Loose locks of thick, dark hair frame a brooding face. His brow steeps heavily over his eyes, casting them in shadow.

Some call him handsome, but to me he seems so typical, so human. He is nothing compared to Calipher's glowing perfection. Why would a demon, who could choose any form he imagined, choose to be something so typical?

"Did something else happen?" he presses.

The heat rushes to my face again. I can't bear to say it out loud.

"Don't you have something else you could do?" The sharpness of my voice stops him in his tracks. He looks down to the dirt, and guilt floods me. I take a breath, ready to apologize.

"Nia?" a velvety voice interrupts from behind us.

My chest seizes. It is Calipher.

My lip trembles as I turn around.

"I didn't mean to," I plead.

At least, I did not mean for him to notice.

For the first time, the peace emanating from him isn't enough. I am distressed beyond its comfort. My fingers beg to touch him again, to let the rush of peace blow away all the bad things inside me. I clutch my hands together to stop myself.

"What is going on?" Bastus steps half in front of me. He has never trusted the angels, not even the one he has worked alongside in this village for so many years. He looks to me. "Nia, what happened?"

He has that look on his face again—an expression that is so much more than concern, a mix of empathy and longing and a strange kind of hunger. It is a look that makes me embarrassed for him, though I have no reason to be.

"Bastus, go."

Bastus glances at me one more time, a reproachful look full of injury. His unsettling aura buzzes through me, competing with Calipher's peaceful one.

"Please," I say. It takes some effort to keep my expression steady while his blank eyes study my face.

He considers, then nods.

He breaks apart into shadow and whooshes away. When the last of his aura stops buzzing through me, I turn to Calipher.

We make our way through the woods side by side. This is all I wanted, to soak up his aura and feel this great calm again. To be close to him. But now distress hums underneath it.

"Why did you do it?" he asks.

My heart races. I can't bear to say it, it is so terribly embarrassing.

"I am so sorry," I whisper.

A tear drops down my cheek, heightening my embarrassment.

But then, Calipher smiles. It is as if the sun has chosen to single me out, of all of the people of the realm. I soak it up as if I have been freezing in the darkness of night all my life.

"There is nothing to apologize for," he says.

I let out a sigh, my throat catching on it from the stress. My mind spins—I am not in trouble? What does he want from me, then?

"But I do wish to know why you did it. Please. Tell me," he says.

I will my eyes to look up again and get lost in his gaze.

When a person is with you, they are right there with you, in that moment only. But angels—it is as if the time and place they are in do not bind them. As if they see something beyond them. Even as Calipher smiles down at me, he seems far away and distant.

Is he listening to Theia? Or to the realm shifting under our feet? The whispers of the trees?

"I...."

How can I possibly explain to him? I am not fully sure myself. I just needed a small piece of his aura so badly. I can't bear his gentle expression any longer and drop my gaze to the forest floor.

"I just needed the peace you give off."

Calipher's smile melts away into a thin, straight line. "Do you not have peace of your own?"

It is like stripping myself naked. "No."

"And when you touched me, did you get the peace you sought?"

"Oh, yes." The unexpected enthusiasm in my voice sounds crass. I bite my lip to stop myself from saying more.

His eyes drift off and his great wings bristle, as if he is lost in great thoughts.

He opens his mouth to speak, and I am afraid of what he will ask next, afraid I will have to explain to him the things in my life that keep peace away. But he doesn't ask.

"When you touched me, I felt something, too," he says. "Something I have never felt before."

My mouth drops open. How could I possibly stir anything in him, this great First Creature of the gods?

For a moment we just stand there, staring at each other.

"Has no one touched you before?"

I realize as I say it just all that means—not one hug, not a friendly stroke of a shoulder, no pressing of hands. And yet, it is not *so* surprising. Most of the people have feared and distrusted him since he arrived. Even the ones who have nothing against him are wary of his other-ness.

But right now, Calipher seems less like a great First Creature and more like a broken bird. His wings are pulled into him tight and his shoulders are tense.

His gaze drifts off, traveling to somewhere far away. I grapple for something else to ask, something to keep him here with me.

"What did it feel like for you, when I touched your wing?"

"It felt like...." He frowns. A sweet crinkle forms between his brows, a single imperfection so beautiful it makes him even more perfect. "It stirred me up. It was like a craving. It was a hunger of the spirit."

It sounds so much like the strained currents that flow through me most of the time. A restless sense that there must be more out there, somewhere. Something better, something good, if only I knew where to look.

I look down, my hair falling from my shoulders and around my face. "I'm so sorry. If I had known my touch would make you feel this way, I would not have done it. I—"

But he stretches his hand out in a gesture to quiet me.

"You misunderstand. This feeling, it was strange. But it was like waking up."

"You...you liked it?" I stutter.

"It was almost as though I had my own Will, outside of Theia's. As if I could become my own being."

I've never fully understood the angels' tie to their goddess. They are individual beings, and yet somehow Theia's Will is planted within them as if it were their own. Is it possible that they do not like it that way?

Confusion clogs my thoughts. I am completely bewildered by this turn of events—the entire morning.

Calipher takes a shy step toward me. "Would you do it again?" he asks.

His request is hesitant and unsure. But his eyes are bright with a fire I've never seen before. It sends feelings coursing through me that I never would have dared to let free.

Would I do it again? If only I never had to stop.

I nod.

He reaches toward me, his palm up. I lay my own over it.

The peace washes over me in a rush, shooting up my arm and nestling into my core. As it fills me it softens, bringing all my anxiety and tension to a standstill, dissolving it into a gentle, pulsing warmth. Underneath it, there is the thrill of touching *him*, this beautiful strange creature that I have longed for, for so long. And this time he is touching me back, craving it as much as I do.

I look up to find he is watching me. I smile. He smiles too, a perfect angelic smile revealing perfect pearl teeth.

And then I do something I had not realized I even wanted.

I don't know what makes me do it, whether it's the relief that he is not angry, or the intense pleasure of his aura, or the giddiness of being here, with him, touching his hand.

But before I can think, I am stretching up to him on my tiptoes, and he is bending his neck down to meet me, and I am pressing my lips into his.

As we connect, his aura hits me so hard I cannot feel the ground beneath me. It is utter perfection.

CHAPTER TWO

WHEN I PULL AWAY from Calipher, a great swelling fear replaces the depths of the aura I felt while kissing him—I should not have done that. Was touching his wing not enough for me? Did I have to ruin it like this? I gasp and turn away.

But Calipher places a hand on my shoulder and turns me back toward him. When I gather my courage to look up at him, he is smiling.

We wander the woods through the rest of the day, and into the night. Our hands entangle as long as we can take the powerful aura rushing through us, then unclasp, only to begin again.

And he kisses me. Again and again and again.

For the first time since my father's Great Illness, I feel cared for. I feel whole. I feel, perhaps, the way I could have, if things had not gone so terribly wrong.

We watch the sun rise from under a tree at the wood's edge, pressed against each other. Then, the magic is over. Calipher must go run his morning prayer, and I have things I must take care of at home.

Before we part ways, he takes my hands. "When can I see you again?"

A thrill tingles down my spine. "This evening?"

He nods, and kisses me one more time before walking away.

The world rushes back with all its cares and burdens. But knowing they will drop away again tonight makes them more bearable.

I float back to the house, my body still buzzing with the afterglow of Calipher's aura. I should be tired, but I'm not. I am too stuffed with peaceful contentedness for that.

Mother is on her way out to tend the field, a slice of bread in her hand. She does not seem to notice that I am just getting home, or the glow I am sure is bursting from me, or that there was no dinner for her last night. It would usually bother me to go so unnoticed by her, but not this morning. I have someone else to notice me now.

I begin by cleaning up the mess left from my fight with Mother yesterday morning. It feels so long ago now, so completely distant from the unexpected lows and highs that have blustered through me since then. So small compared to my long walk through the night with Calipher.

Once the house is back in order, I pull out the store of grains from the fields that we keep for ourselves, and begin baking fresh loaves of bread.

I give myself over to the rhythm of kneading the dough. But Calipher's kisses still linger on my lips, and my mind keeps drifting back to the path in the woods. I lose myself in daydreams until a sharp knock at the door jolts me out of it. I am just putting a loaf in the fiery-hot oven, and I flinch, burning my arm on the iron.

"By the gods!" I curse.

As I approach the door, a familiar uneasiness seeps into me, fighting for the space where Calipher's peace is nestled inside my chest.

"Bastus."

I hold the door open with my foot, my hand busy wrapping a wet cloth over my burn.

Bastus bursts through it and stops abruptly, our bodies just inches apart. His piercing blank eyes are electric with concern, and his full lips press tensely against each other. He towers a full head over me.

"Nia, why did you not tell me? I never would have left you with him, had I known." His voice crackles with urgency.

The lean muscles of his shoulders are tense and his fists are clutched tight at his sides.

"Tell you what?"

His icy blue eyes narrow. "You should have told me what happened in the village with Calipher, about touching his wing."

A prick of embarrassment pierces my chest. "How did you find out about that?"

"All the village is speaking of it."

I moan and press my forehead against the side of the door.

"Well?" he prompts. "Are you all right? Did he do that to you?" he asks, pointing to the cloth wrapped around my burned arm.

"Of course not. You did that to me more than he did."

The panicked expression that rolls over him is satisfying. I do not know why I make things so difficult for him. He means well. But his concern is like a weed that grows too fast to be cut back, always growing back twice as strong.

I laugh, trying to lighten the mood. "I just meant you startled me when you knocked. I burned myself on the oven is all."

He leans forward and removes the cloth from the burn to look at it. "I am sorry."

The burn's sting returns under his gaze. I take the cloth out of his hand and cover it again.

"It's really not that bad."

He turns his frown on me again. "Nia, what's going on? People in the village are saying you angered him. That he chased you into the woods and has not been seen since. They're using words like 'wrath' and 'fury.'"

"That's not what happened." I say it through gritted teeth.

"But...." His icy flat eyes scrutinize me. "*Something* happened?"

"I touched his wing." Saying it to Bastus, it feels like a confession. A betrayal of some sort. "But he was not angry with me."

I don't want to talk about it. What happened after, in the woods, I want it to stay my own sweet secret. Talking about Calipher and what happened between us will bring it into the light, leave it vulnerable to judgment. Especially with Bastus.

"Bastus, I need you to go."

I start to close the door.

"Wait!" His fingers wrap over the door's latch. "You touched Calipher's wing in the marketplace yesterday. What happened after? To go by what they are saying in the village, he dragged you away in a fury."

"He did no such thing. For the love of the gods, Bastus, you were there when Calipher caught up to me. Did he appear full of rage to you? I know you did not think so then, or you would never have left me with him."

That much I can say for Bastus. He always looks out for me.

"Nia, please. Tell me what happened." His mouth tightens at the corners, tense with concern and something else I do not want to acknowledge.

"Come on, Bastus. I have work to do. Do you not, as well?"

"Riamne."

I hate when he uses my full name. No one else does, not since my father. It was his mother's name.

"What does it matter to you, Bastus?"

His forehead knits together. He reaches out as if to touch my arm and the unsettling buzz of his aura grows greater as he nears, but then pulls away again.

"You know, Nia. Surely you do."

He takes a half-step toward me, his lip trembling with emotion that his flat eyes refuse to echo. The space between us grows tense, and I step back to escape it, my eyes dropping to the floor. It is dusty. I will need to clean it this afternoon. I focus on that, allow it to distract me from what I do not want to admit.

His aura wrestles through me and amplifies the discomfort his words stir within me. I wish he would just go. But he will not go until he knows what happened. I sigh.

"I touched his wing in the market. I was embarrassed and ran off, which is when you saw me. He followed after me, and we talked. And then....," I swallow. "I kissed him."

"You kissed him?" Bastus snaps. He closes his eyes for a moment and takes a moment to calm himself. He looks back to me. "What then?"

"Well. He kissed me back."

"Oh, Nia."

His disappointment stings. But then a swell of resentment flares in me and pushes it out. This is not his to judge. He has no claim on me. I have half a mind to slam the door on him.

He leans in closer.

"Do you understand why I have never asked you to be mine, Nia? Because even the god of Chaos has a few rules that are not to be broken."

I stiffen. Hot embers of anger ignite within me, and his unsettling aura fans the flames.

"No. You haven't asked because you know what I would say. But I can't stop living my life to spare your feelings."

As soon as the words escape me, the full weight of them sinks in. I want to reach out and catch them so I can hide them away. But it is too late. Bastus' expression drains. A tight ball of muscle hardens in his jaw as it clenches. I am sure he is about to explode.

My cheeks grow hot and guilt stirs within me. All I want is to cling to what is left of Calipher's aura, and right now it's getting buried under Bastus.

I step back and close the door on him. As I do, I catch a glimpse of him breaking apart into shadow and whooshing away.

I lean back against the door and shut my eyes. I try desperately to shove the guilt away and draw the warm hum of Calipher's aura back out, but it is gone.

Chapter Three

Even after Bastus and his restless aura are gone, the warm, bubbling bliss from last night is diminished, and I can't coax it back.

I want it back. And I do not want to wait for this evening.

I stop kneading dough and pile the cooling loaves into a basket while I wait for the one in the oven to finish. I'll need to go to the village to trade anyway; I might as well go now. Calipher is always in the village center through the morning.

When I reach the village, I look around for him, but he is nowhere to be seen. Perhaps someone required his assistance.

Impatience tugs at my heart.

I busy myself with my trades for tonight's dinner.

Around me people move with unusual focus, and there is less chatter through the village center. More whispering and significant looks. Who knew such a small village could hold so many opinions in it?

What is it to me if the village wants to judge? Nothing, I tell myself. It is nothing new for them to keep their distance from me.

I take my time, but even so it only takes but a few moments to complete. Still Calipher is nowhere.

I turn and wander by Shara and her butcher's stand. Even when the village feared us most, right after my father's death, when I was young and learning to trade in his stead, Shara has always been kind to me. She is usually generous with the village's latest gossip, too. I pause to inspect today's cuts, wait for her to address me.

"Morning's greetings, Nia," she says.

"And to you," I reply, as casually as I can. "How was morning prayer?"

Her smile disappears. "You haven't heard?"

My hand folds into an anxious ball. "Heard what?"

"There was, well, an unexpected visitor." She raises her eyebrows.

We hardly ever get visitors from other places here. "At prayer? At Calipher's prayer?"

"Another angel."

There has never been more than one angel assigned to a town. Only very few of us have ever even seen an angel other than Calipher, just a few of the traders who travel to other villages often.

Shara shakes her head, eyes wide. "She appeared at the end of prayer. She walked through us as if we were not even there, right to Calipher. And then they went out toward the woods."

A knot tangles in my stomach.

"Why is she here?"

"I don't know," she says. "But she looked angry."

Shara glances at me as she speaks, shifting her feet. Even many of the gods' most committed followers never got comfortable with the First Creatures among us. Shara is no exception.

"Which way did they go?"

Her eyes widen. "I don't think you should—"

"Which way?"

I know what she is thinking—that after my antics yesterday, it is my fault there is another angel among us.

Shara points. "Back toward his home."

I head off in the same direction, searching for them as I go. My heart pounds and my blood rushes as I reach Calipher's little home. It is no more than a twist of oversized tree roots that Theia grew into a home just for him, but also infinitely special because of that fact. Branches tower over it, shading it, making the powerful glow emanating from it seem even greater. Along with the light, strong waves of peace waft out, even from a distance.

I hesitate, unsure if I should go any closer.

There is no reason to fear a pair of angels—they are beings of peace—and yet something very serious must have happened for another angel to be here.

I am about to turn away and leave when the door flies open. I almost run to it before I realize the light is not silvery like Calipher, but golden, almost like the sun. It is the other angel.

Shara was right. The angel is tall, with generous curves. She has rosy-gold hair that tumbles in soft curls past her shoulders and gleams like a sunset. Her wings rustle as her eyes meet mine, her thin lips pursed together into a stern pout.

I stumble back a step. Her beauty is daunting in its perfection, and I feel small and insignificant in comparison.

"You must be the reason I was sent here," she declares. Her voice is like the roar of a waterfall. "There is nothing here for you, girl. Go, and do not come back."

Were the townspeople right to blame me?

I gape, startled at her splendor and torn between fleeing and rushing past her into Calipher's arms.

"C-Calipher?" I call, but it comes out weak and is swallowed in the glow.

I can make out a vague silvery glow behind the door, but he does not respond, or even move. I want to run to him, but I am too frightened.

"Go."

The angel's voice rolls like a bear's growl, and her lips form a scowl that bares her teeth.

My stomach twists, and I hurry away, afraid of what the angel will do to me if I don't, and even more afraid of what she has in store for Calipher.

Chapter Four

I RUN ALL THE way home, heedless of the slapping branches and grabbing underbrush. Was Bastus right? Is being together really so offensive to the gods?

I step into the hearth and set my basket down. My anxieties have pushed out almost all of what was left of Calipher's aura. The need for sleep wallops me.

I go straight to bed. Mother won't notice or care, not in the state she's in. I flop against my pillow, and drift away immediately.

What feels like just minutes later, I am awakened with a rough shake.

"Are you *mad*?"

I moan and open my eyes, startled and stiff.

Mother stands over me. It would be wonderful to see her being herself again, if she weren't frowning at me so severely.

I rub my eyes. "What?"

How long was I sleeping? Outside the window, the sun is already setting.

"Are you *mad*?" Mother repeats. "Touching an angel's wing?"

She storms away, swings her arms in anger, and begins pacing the room. There is no point in trying to defend myself until she is done.

"Why would you do such a thing? What were you thinking?"

I clench my fists to keep from yelling back at her. "Where did you hear this gossip, from the farmhands? You don't know—"

"I know enough. You spend all your time with Firsts."

"And what's wrong with that?"

I already know. We've had this argument a thousand times over. But as the sluggishness of sleep wears off, my familiar anger toward her roars in my stomach. I want her to feel it, too.

"The Firsts are a deception," she roars. "They are useless meddlers."

They couldn't save my father, she means.

I wonder if she knows the extent to which Calipher and I are—*were*—involved. But it doesn't matter now.

"But—"

She slams a fist into the wall. I hate when she is like this, but it is not as bad as when she disappears into herself.

"You will stop this, Nia. You will stay away from that angel."

"I will do as I see fit!" I am screaming now, tears welling in my eyes for no particular reason, determined to simply be heard.

There is no reason for this, a small, rational voice whispers in my head. It's over anyway. It barely even began.

But she never let go of what Calipher did when Father was fading away from us. Theia ordered him back to his other duties, and he went. He did not have a choice, with Her Will within him.

Bastus and Peri too eventually needed to tend to their other duties.

Father had been a devout follower of Theia since he was a child. For Theia's ambassador to us to turn away—for Mother, it was the final betrayal, the ultimate proof that the First Creatures were not truly in this realm for our benefit, as so many had suspected.

Mother gives me her most menacing look, her shoulders quivering. "You will obey me, Nia."

"I am grown now, Mother. You can't hold me back forever simply because Father is no longer here."

And then I storm out of the house.

I burst into the twilight and head toward the fields. Mother doesn't bother to call after me. I need to walk, to be out, so that I might think.

My chest churns with anger.

I usually love to walk the fields at night. If I were not so distraught, it would be a good night for it. The moon is full and proud, and a quiet breeze blows.

Bastus hates when I wander around in the dark like this. He says I am vulnerable out here all alone. But vulnerable to what, I could not say. He speaks sometimes as if men are not so good after all, as if there is an evil out there waiting to lure us in.

But this young world is perfect and lovely and peaceful, and there is no reason to fear. I often tell him so, and he purses his lips.

I wonder what Calipher would say.

A rustle of steps in the brush behind me takes me out of the thoughts—*right on cue.*

"Bastus, let me be." I say it reflexively, without thinking.

"It is not Bastus."

The voice is soft like velvet. My heart lurches in my chest.

I turn around.

"Calipher!"

I rush toward him, eager for his touch, but he flinches back and pushes his hands out: *Stop.*

It's like being hit in my gut. How can he ask me to stay away after yesterday?

"Is that other angel still here?"

The ting of his peaceful aura hums just under my skin. I want more.

"No."

"Who was she? Why was she here?" My voice begins to quiver, so I choke back the rest of my questions. I do not want him to see how afraid I really am.

"Theia sent her," he replies. "She had a warning for me."

His wings slouch behind his shoulders. It has the effect of making him look like a candle, slowly melting away under a flame.

"A warning?" Suddenly my throat feels dry and tight. "What kind of warning?"

"It was about us," he says. He looks away. "About yesterday. Nia, we can't keep on like this."

"But...." His words seep into me, and they sting. "It was so wonderful. Did you not think so too?"

"Yes." The word comes out broken, as if it is a struggle for him. "Wonderful. But that is not what matters. It is Theia's Will. The angel came to remind me to keep my distance from you and the other humans."

A completely new kind of anger bursts free in me. It is raw and feral and burns through my core. Heat flares over my face.

"But what about you? She can't just order you to stop feeling. You have a right to your own choice."

He shakes his head. "For you, for humans, free will is a right. For angels, it is nothing. I do not get free will. I have Theia's Will. Today, Her Will is for me to keep away from you.

"But," I start, hardly knowing what I'll say next, determined to argue this away, "if She is making you stay away from me, how are you here?"

Calipher pauses, a puzzled frown flickering over his face.

"I do not know. I had to explain to you. Abandoning you without doing so did not feel like an option. And here I am."

He takes half a step forward, slowly, as if testing himself. I start toward him as well, his aura building in me as I near, but then he draws back again.

"I must leave," he says. His words bear the weight of thick storm clouds about to burst open.

He looks at me, and I can almost feel my heart shattering.

"I will keep my distance from you, and I ask you to do the same, for both our sakes."

I grasp for words, but there are none.

Of the three gods, Theia has always felt cold and distant to me, too removed from this realm She helped to create. But even so, I cannot imagine how She can do this.

"I am sorry, Nia."

His voice reverberates inside me. I bite my lip and try to soak up the stillness of his aura while I can.

He wraps his wings around himself, and in a blink, he has disappeared.

Tears build in my eyes, but I force them to stay open and take in every bit of him that I can. Was there always a black feather among the brilliant silver?

I shake myself and try to pull myself together. I am not losing anything, not really—it has hardly been a day. I have no right to the feelings raging through me.

But, oh, how I crave his touch, that divine peace that blasts through him. It was like nothing else in this world, and losing it is too much to bear.

I trudge back home, too empty to care about the fight with Mother anymore.

Chapter Five

I try to go about my days. I tidy the house, I clean the dishes. I trade in the market. I prepare the meals. But Calipher is always at the forefront of my mind. The warm peace he filled me with is gone, replaced with the angry burning coals that usually simmer within me. It is not enough.

How could he just leave me?

Not him. Theia did this, I remind myself.

But the anger is crackling and simmering inside me anyway. It does not matter whose fault it is. What matters is that yesterday I had something beautiful, and it was snatched away from me.

Calipher seems to go about his usual duties, lending counsel, visiting the ill, and otherwise guiding the village to remain in harmony with the gods.

But ever since the other angel came to the village, people have been worse than normal. They keep their distance and lean to each other, whispering, when I pass. Even Cyril, who was such a good friend of my father's before he died, has stopped making small talk with me when I come to trade.

I am glad for it, I decide. I have no energy for the effort of meaningless chatter, and prefer to simply do what I must and return home, where I can let myself drown in Calipher's absence alone.

A quick, light knock at the door interrupts my stupor.

I rub my eyes dry and answer it.

A diminutive creature with full cheeks and cornhusk-blonde ringlets is waiting for me.

"Peri!"

Peri is a sprite, sent to the village by Gloros, goddess of the passions. She came to us shortly after Calipher and Bastus.

She is a lively thing, and her large eyes are always full of joy. Combined with her small stature, as a child I often forgot that she was not the same age as me. She spent endless time with me in the fields playing games, and caring for me, when my mother was too buried in grief to do it herself. When we played hide and seek, her greenish tint could make her impossible to find in the woods. Unlike angels' full feathery wings, hers are delicate like petals.

Peri's aura ignites and magnifies emotions. But she can also reduce it, and as a child she used this to protect me from my grief, allowing me to digest my father's death in bites small enough for a child to take. Then over time she weaned me off it, fading out of my life. There were others to tend to.

It would be good to see her, if her presence were not multiplying my sadness so that it felt like it would burst from my chest.

She gives me an apologetic half-smile.

"Bastus sent me. He was afraid you would not want to speak to him."

I still have not spoken to Bastus since our fight. I haven't even seen him since then, I realize. Has he been avoiding me on purpose?

"Oh."

Peri's wings twitch. "May I?"

"Of course." I step aside and let her in. "What can I do for you? Or, for Bastus?"

"I—he—*we* were just worried about you. The village...."

"Yes, I know what they are saying."

They whisper, but they forget to keep their voices down. I hear when they observe that I do not look well, that I brought trouble upon this village, that perhaps I have been struck with my father's illness for it. I hear when they question what I could be doing with those First Creature males so often, all on our own.

"It's been hard, long years for you." Peri's frown reaches her large eyes, reflecting back all my troubles.

"I've gotten used to it." I wander the kitchen, rearranging and setting things in place as an excuse to turn away.

Peri reaches up and places her little hand on my arm. The magnification of my heartache is instant. "That does not make it all right."

I shrug away from her and breathe in relief. "It is what it is."

"You should come out more in the town. If you were out more, the people would get past this," she suggests. "You need distraction. Community."

"I do not mind being alone." But I realize as I say it, this is less true now than it used to be.

Peri smiles. "Even so. Why not try coming to morning prayer? Your father still has many old friends there."

I shrug and nod. Maybe.

"Think about it." Peri sighs. "Is there anything you wish to talk about?"

"No."

She pauses, then turns toward the door.

"Except...."

She turns back, her wings perking up.

"Could you do that thing you used to? After my father?"

"Oh." She slouches back down, biting her lip in apprehension. "You were a child then, and not ready for all that was put on you."

She sighs, weighing her decision. I slouch, try to show her the full weight of my depression.

"That is not a way to fix things, Nia. You know that?"

"Yes, yes, I know. I just need a break from it, is all."

She sighs again, and nods. "Just this once."

"Thank you," I exclaim. I lean forward, and she flutters her wings to raise herself up to me.

She presses her thumb into my forehead, and a satisfying hum rushes through me, blocking out my heartache like a shield.

"Thank you," I whisper, smiling at her.

She nods, her eyes full of concern. "I'm around, Nia. So is Bastus. If you need anything, don't just wither away here. Come to us."

And then she leaves.

Peri's idea of a prayer service sticks in my mind. It feels surprisingly appealing.

But I cannot go to Peri's prayer. Even thinking about it reminds me too much of my father, of better times for all of us before his Great Illness. To feel all that, in addition to my heartache, multiplied by Peri's presence, it is too much to even think about.

Bastus' prayer is out, too, after our last fight. His feelings for me grew like a weed between us. For years we ignored them, but now he has put words to them. Now that he is gone, I realize he has been my dearest friend, and his absence has left a hole in my spirit. But I do not know how to be around him right now.

Usually the gods complement and balance each other, but now it is as if they are each taking a limb and pulling me in a different direction. Pulling me apart.

These days, there is only one thing I am drawn toward. But Calipher asked me to stay away.

I tell myself it will get better. But every day I only become more weary. I need to be in his presence again, even if only to soak him up from a distance.

So, finally, I give in and go to one of Calipher's morning prayers for Theia's followers. Leading us in our worship of the gods is one of the First Creatures' main duties here among us, along with counsel and helping us to live in harmony with the realm.

My heart throbs in my ears the whole way there. They meet outside in the forest by Calipher's home, no matter the weather.

He sees me as I approach the group, and his usual calm, distant expression shifts. Is that sadness I see in his eyes? Anger? I cannot tell.

This was a mistake. I shouldn't be here. I almost walk away. But I can already feel the warmth of his aura, and it makes me whole again. So instead I walk right to him.

His lips spread in a slow, guarded smile. "It seems Theia may be able to keep me away from you, but not even a god can keep you away from me."

"No," I say. I look away, feeling guilty for approaching him at all. "It seems She can't. I just wanted you to know, I'm coming to prayer. I need it, Calipher, or I wouldn't be doing this. But I intend to respect your request. I'll stay to the back."

He is close enough that his aura saturates me like I am floating a lake of it. Close enough that that I could reach out and touch him.

"All are welcome to prayer. Always." He forces the edges of his mouth up into a stiff smile.

"Thank you."

I will myself to turn away and move to the back of the group, like I promised. Theia's followers whisper and glare as I make my way through them, but I am getting used to it, and it does not bother me. It just feels so good to be near him again.

I try to focus on the prayer service. But I was never here for Theia, and She is not what I need. My mind keeps drifting to the soft glow of his skin, the gentle curls of his hair, the way his lips felt on mine. Not even the waves of peace that flow off of him are enough to quench me. Not now. I sit still and quiet on the dewy ground and soak up as much as of him as I can.

His eyes keep drifting to me as he addresses the crowd—the flicker of an intense stare, and then he moves on to the rest of them. Every time goosebumps rise over my arms.

The service is over before I am ready. The others begin to shift and speak again, and I realize it is time to go. I close my eyes and take in one last moment, then turn and make myself leave, afraid that if I do not keep my promise well enough, I will not be allowed to keep coming.

I start down the path home, but a rustle in the branches makes me look back. Calipher is emerging from the brush.

"Wait," he calls to me. I do. He steps out of the brush, but doesn't come any closer. "You do not need to keep to the back when you come to prayer. Come as much as you like, sit where you like, and do not worry about me."

My feet move to close the space between us. I go slowly, afraid he will flee if I rush him. But he stays where he is and allows me to approach.

"I miss you," I whisper.

"Nia...." his voice trails off to nothing. He shakes his head. He starts as if to lean toward me, then stumbles a step back.

I step forward again and close the space between us. Then I rise up on my tiptoes, grab onto his robe to pull him down to me, and I kiss him.

At first he is stiff with surprise, but then to my relief he kisses back. He kisses me with an anxious hunger, over and over again, deep and hard and fast. He lifts me up to him and I wrap my arms and legs around him. Pressed up against him like this, his aura is more powerful than ever. Tidal waves of deep contentment crash over me. It is like nothing I have ever experienced—more powerful, more real, more wonderful.

I crave more of it.

I slip his robe off his shoulders to see what he'll do. He keeps kissing me, covering my face and neck. So I keep going, push the clothing away from his perfect marble skin. Then I start on my own robe.

He drops me to my feet and pulls away.

"We shouldn't...." His protest is only a whisper, hot and restless.

"I'm tired of doing what I should," I say. "It has worn me out. Do you *want* to?"

He digests my words.

"Not here," he says, nodding to the others leaving from prayer not far away through the trees. "Hold on tight."

Before I can realize what is happening, he has whisked me into his arms and we are soaring up toward the sky. I cling to him and look down, in awe at how small everything is below us. I can see the village, the forest, my home, and the field. The wind blasts all around us. It's an amazing feeling.

Our descent back to the earth is gentler. We land in a mountain over the forest. A waterfall bubbles near us, feeding into the river that rushes down the mountain's side and past the town.

He lays me down on the ground next to it, his arms staying in place around me, and leans forward until I am on the earth below him.

His breaths are heaving. At first I think it is from carrying me here. But while his eyes are eager and tender, his face is grimaced, as if straining against something. *Theia's Will*, I realize with a pang of understanding. *He's fighting against it to be here with me.*

I pull him in and kiss him, then untie my robe. The waterfall splatters over us in a mist, tickling on my arms and raising goosebumps over my skin. He wraps his arms around me and lays me out on the grass again.

He moves urgently. Anxiously. He kisses every inch of me with his cool, marble lips. When he moves inside me, it is like nothing I have ever experienced, an intensity of his aura I didn't know was possible, like my very skin is alight with a deep happiness that should not even be possible. It intensifies every touch, every brush of skin, every press of lips. It is as if I am floating through the sky on a cloud of it, until finally it overcomes me and I crest.

As he watches me, Calipher gasps sharply into my shoulder, and his wings stretch out rigidly to their full span. With the sun shining over them, I am surrounded by glistening silver.

After, we linger, sprawled over the grass, and bask in the afterglow of the moment. Calipher relaxes his wings back in halfway, so that they wrap around us like a canopy and shields us from the world.

I sigh. There is nothing like this buzzing perfection in all the realms.

But his breathing is still heavy, and getting worse.

"Calipher." I hate to break the moment's perfection, but I need to know. "What is it doing to you, to be here with me? This was perfect. If I could stay here forever with you, I would. But how is it that you can be here?"

"There is a force urging me away," he says. "But I wanted it, I wanted *you*. I wanted you so badly. I have never wanted something for myself before. But *you*...you make me feel like I can do anything I choose."

He traces a finger idly over my waist.

"When I saw you this morning, I could feel Her commanding me to push you away, but I could not do it. I just could not bear to do it, and so I did not."

I pull him in and kiss him. I am so full of wonderful feelings I am sure I will burst. But under them there is a twinge of nerves near my heart. I press a hand into his chest.

"Does it hurt?"

"No."

I raise an eyebrow. "I do not believe you."

He only smiles in response.

"Is Theia going to send that other angel back?"

He traces a line from my temple, down the side of my face and my neck. "I don't know," he says, leaning forward to kiss my shoulder. "And I do not care. Do not worry about it, my Nia."

He smiles.

My Nia. His. I do not think I could feel any more full of happiness.

We float in the buzz of our mingling auras a while longer, until Calipher confesses he must yield to the pull. When we finally get up, we are woozy from the power coursing through us.

I cannot help watching him as he pulls his robe back on, perfect and glowing.

That is when I see the speckles on his great silver wings. There are more splotches of darkness in them than I realized before.

"How are some of your feathers dark, when all the rest are silver?" I ask.

"But they are all silver," he says. He twists around, and then he sees it, too. He frowns. "How strange."

I giggle, but he keeps staring at it, his frown burrowing a small wrinkle between his brows.

I finish tying my robe and leap to him, wrapping my arms around him and taking in the warm peace. "They're perfect. Like the rest of you."

CHAPTER SIX

IT HAS BEEN TOO long since we had rain. In the village, people are fretting over the crops, wondering what we have done to anger the gods now. Sometimes their eyes drift toward me as they speak of it.

I hold my head high and pretend I do not see it. But inside I am wracked with guilt. The rain has not come since the day before Calipher and I went to the river together.

Calipher says the Three do not work that way. That Theia would not punish everyone for our wrongdoing. That She wouldn't even control the weather directly in the first place, or by Herself.

"But then why has the rain stopped?"

I lie over a bed of leaves deep in the forest, the only refuge from the sun's angry heat.

He smiles, a gentle, perfect smile that dimples at his chin, and kisses me. "Do not fret over it, my love."

I wish I were as sure as Calipher is that we are not causing the drought. But it has been a week, and there has been no response to our continued trysts.

He pushes a swell of his aura on me, urging me to relax into it. It is easy not to worry when I am with him.

Our robes dangle over a nearby branch. Even next to the river, with no rain and no clouds to cool the earth, it is too hot for clothes. He turns over and lays his head on my stomach.

I breathe in deeply, then let the air out slowly, arching my back. Calipher nestles in and kisses my breast in response. I close my eyes and try to let his aura fill me. But its pull over me isn't as strong as I remember it that first time in the market.

That certainly doesn't seem to be the case for Calipher. If anything, he seems to feel the energy he gains from me more than ever. Something has started to shift behind his eyes. That eternal calm is fading, and they are becoming busier. More curious, more distracted, more alive. I wish I felt his aura as strongly as mine seems to fuel him. But it makes my heart flutter with pleasure to see him like this, to think that it is because of me.

I sigh and stretch out, run my fingers through his hair. He is right; I should relax.

But then something shifts, the air tightens and crackles. I pull myself up onto my elbow to see. Calipher springs to his feet. Another angel appears near us, already approaching at a brisk pace.

It is the same one as before, her glow brilliant like the sun. She ignores our nudity and walks right to Calipher, her expression stormy. When she is close enough, she reaches out and presses her thumb into his forehead. She murmurs a chant I cannot hear. Calipher looks startled for a flash, and then his face goes blank.

"Calipher! Calipher!"

I try to reach for him but the angel stretches out her other hand toward me, and I cannot move.

"Calipher!" I shriek. My heart pound in my ears.

As the angel turns away, she gives me the slightest of smiles, one that is cold and callous. She strides away into the trees and disappears as if she has slipped behind a curtain.

"What did you do!" I scream after her.

But I fear I already know.

When I turn back to him, he is already dressed and spreading his wings to fly away.

I want to call after him, but it catches in my throat with a sob. As he soars off, the peace he filled me with fades to nothing. In its place a wave of dread comes over me and settles deep into my bones. I fear I have lost him for good this time.

I dress myself, and then wander the forest, making my way slowly back down the mountain. We were farther out than I realized.

I prefer flying.

When I finally reach home, Mother is sitting on the step outside. When she sees me, she stops tapping on the step and stands, folding her arms across her chest.

"Where exactly have *you* been?" She is covered in dirt and sweat head to toe. Her arms are folded over her chest.

"Out."

"And what by the gods does that mean? I have been lugging jugs from the river to the fields with the other farmers since sunrise. I am hungry. "

I almost apologize on reflex, but her tone riddles my heart with resentment. Could she not have found her own meal just once?

"Dinner will be ready soon."

"Where have you been?" she demands again.

I do not have it in me, after my long trek down the mountain, to argue. My spirit is already in shreds.

I turn away from her and fire up the oven, determined to hold onto the last embers of Calipher's aura and not let her stomp it out.

"Were you with that angel?"

I whip around and stare at her. "Where did you hear that from?"

Do they all know? Not that it matters now. Still, guilt flares within me in hot splotches.

"So it is true."

She is still standing. Standing and glaring at me like I've taken something from her. Her hands curl into fists and the veins of her forearms raise against the muscle.

"Where did you hear that?" I repeat.

How I crave Calipher's calming touch now. What I would give to stroke his feathers again and feel that rush of perfect peace.

Mother rolls her eyes. "In the drought we all work together to keep the fields watered. You think I do not hear them talking? They think the drought is because of you."

"That is ridiculous. It is Father all over again. I am not going to let rumors dictate my choices."

Calipher said the gods wouldn't do that. I cling to his promise and hope it is the truth. Could an angel lie, if he wanted to?

"Do not speak of your father. That angel you have been out doing gods know what with all day, he walked away and let him die."

"You know that's not true. He did all he could, all the Firsts did. He left because he could do nothing. To let us have our time with him before he was gone."

She stomps her foot, creating a loud *thunk* as it slams into the wooden floor.

"You will not see him again."

The words burn right through me. I hate when she uses my full name. It slices my heart and out of it floods a hot pulsing rage. But it is true—I won't see him again. Theia has taken him back.

"You will not start telling me what to do. Not now. Years ago I could have used that. When I was a child. But I'm not a child anymore, and now I choose for myself."

"I had to care for my husband!"

"Care for him? What care did you provide? You fretted by him and blamed everyone around you, and left no room for anything else. *You chose him over me.*"

I can hardly believe my own mouth. We have gone too deep now. I am saying the things I have kept buried inside me for years, things I have kept to myself because to say them would be useless, to say them would only be to hurt. But I want to hurt her now, I want her to feel the way I feel—raw, burned, empty.

"You are still choosing him over me, and I am the only one still here."

She stumbles back and blinks, as if she has been hit in the face. The rage is still simmering in her eyes but she stutters for words that aren't there.

I shove a plate of bread and dried meats at her and put out the stove fire—I can't stand to be here long enough to cook now. Then I storm out, making sure to slam the door as loudly as possible.

After pacing alongside the fields for a while, I start to calm down. I start to regret what I said. I would go back and apologize if it would make any difference. But it is out now, and there is no way to take it back.

Besides, I meant every word of it.

As I pace through the fields, rain begins to fall.

CHAPTER SEVEN

THE RAIN KEEPS COMING every night. The thick heat clears, and the farmers stop having to haul water to the fields all day. A breeze cuts the sun's strength like the realm is sighing from relief.

That morning at prayer, I look up to find myself caught in Calipher's gaze. His face is completely blank and his eyes are strained, as if he is grappling for something he has forgotten. As soon as the meeting is over I try to approach him—how much does he remember? But as I get close he flinches, and then his great wings spread and he flies away from me. As he grows small against the sky, a desperate ache tugs at my chest.

A rise of murmurs bring my attention back to the worshipers, and I realize they were watching the whole thing. Tears well in my eyes, and I run past them toward home.

I stop going after that. It hurts too much to go now, and see him with his followers. I do not try to speak to him—I know he will not be the same.

I only see him in the village now, on the rare occasion when I am not quick enough to miss him. I had not noticed before, drunk on his aura, how he had changed. The lines of his face seem deeper somehow, and his shoulders slump in a way that suggests he bears a great weight. The tips of his wings have turned black as midnight.

How I crave to run into his arms and let the deep peace of his aura swell within me.

Every night I go walking in the fields in the rain, too restless to sleep. I walk until I am too exhausted to move anymore, and only then do I make my way back and collapse onto the bed, finally numbed by exhaustion.

"Nia."

It is Calipher's perfect smooth voice. Hearing him say my name is like coming home. My heart pounds in sync with the pattering of the rain.

What is he doing out here?

"Calipher...I can't. Please just go away."

To speak with him as if everything we were has been erased... I don't think my heart could bear it.

"Nia. Please."

It is so deceptive, his voice. Just like before, so warm and full of feeling.

But even now, when he's just a shell of his former self, I can't say no to him. I turn around.

The rain trickles over him, and his perfect curls are tousled and matted. His wings are tense and slightly spread around him like a dark halo. In the shadow, he glows like a warm fire, and I want to curl up to him.

But as I look closer, what I notice are his eyes. The filmed distance, the unfocused stare, it's gone. They are sharp and alert, fixed on me with wild desperation. He's panting, as if he is physically strained.

"Calipher?"

"My love." He rushes into me and squeezes me tight. "I'm sorry, I'm sorry, I'm sorry, I'm sorry." The same two words, over and over and over, a waterfall begging forgiveness.

"Shhhhh." I stroke his hair back away from his face, and then run my fingers over his lips to quiet him. "It is not your fault."

He pulls back slightly to look at me, his face just inches from mine.

"Oh, gods, how I have missed you."

He kisses me, long and desperately. He kisses me over and over and over, hardly giving me time to breathe. But I don't care. I don't need air, I need him. I need him more than I've ever needed anything. I tell him so.

In response, he kisses me even more, even harder. He covers my face, my neck, my shoulders in them, his mouth wild and hungry, his hands traveling up and down my body, as if trying to hold all of me at once.

Overhead, a rumble of thunder rolls over the sky.

"It is going to storm." Even as I say it, the raindrops get heavier.

Calipher lifts me into his arms and we fly away, into the covered protection of the woods. As soon as we land he presses me against the trunk of a tree and hurriedly continues where we left off. His wings are dripping and spread wide, drops running over the feathers and dripping from the tips. He's rigid and pulsing against me, and I crave him. I have to be as close to him as I possibly can.

He's already pulling my wet robe off to get to me, running his hands over my breasts and up my thighs, which are clenched tight against his sides.

All through the storm we make love. Rough and desperate and craving. His mouth is open against my arm, my shoulder, my neck, his teeth press into me like he needs to consume me, like even being pressed against me isn't close enough. I dig my nails into his back, straining to bring him closer, closer, closer. Our wet skin glistens against the lightning, slips against each other's. He presses against me in a way that is almost frantic. My back digs into the tree's bark behind me, but I'm too elated to care about a few scratches.

When the storm is over and the first rays of sun stretch free through the clouds, my robe and my body are both in tatters. I see the little bruises and imprints of teeth showing themselves in splotches over my body, but I can't find it in me to care. I'm too brimming over with his aura, too happy and relieved to have him back.

He presses one last kiss into my forehead. "I will see you tonight."

"Promise?" I beg. I do not want to let him go. Not ever.

"Promise."

I stumble home, half exhausted, half drunk on his aura. Mother is already gone for the day, and I drop right into bed.

Chapter Eight

I wake up dreaming of Calipher's fluttering wings and the coolness of his body pressed against me.

I get through my morning chores as quickly as I can. I don't want to see my mother, I just want to hold on to the sweet feelings I woke up with.

Then I go outside. The morning is still damp from yesterday's storm. It really was a heavy one—branches are strewn all over, and the crops look like they took a beating. But they're still standing. A couple of early birds sing to the sky.

A feeling swells within me—a great peacefulness. I turn to look around, and there he his. Calipher is waiting for me just to the side of our house.

"Good morning." My smile is so big it pulls in my cheeks. But when I move toward him and reach out my arms, he flinches and steps back.

"I can't," he says.

"But—"

His face scrunches and he snaps at me, "Stop. I have to say something important, and it's my only chance."

He has never snapped at me before. Not once.

My smile washes away. Something cold and dark twists through my stomach. "What is it?"

"I have to go back to the Host."

The coldness rises and swallows my heart.

"I am so sorry. I did not mean to get you in trouble again." I reach out reflexively to comfort him, but he pulls further away. "When will I see you again?"

His head droops, and he mumbles into his chest, "You won't."

The flames inside me are doused out and I turn numb. "I do not understand."

"I will not be coming back."

"Oh, come now." I laugh, trying to keep it together. Trying to get my head around it all. "Theia has tried to keep us apart. You always come back to me."

"I'm not coming back, Nia."

Tears well up in my eyes. It can't be true.

"But—"

"Nia." He lunges forward and shakes me. "I don't have long. I need you to listen."

I close my mouth and bite my lip.

"I love you, Nia. More than I've ever loved anything, more than I ever could love anything again. I don't want you to miss me. I want you to be happy. Even if…." He loses his thought for a moment. "Even if it means finding someone else. So I made something for you."

He digs into his robe and pulls out a necklace, which he holds out to me in his palm. It's gold and glistening, the most beautiful thing I've ever seen, other than him. Dangling from the chain, there is a large emerald stone. Unlike most jewels, this one is still raw and uncut, as if pulled right from where it grew.

"Wear this, and you will always have a piece of me with you. You will always be loved."

I shake my head. The tears roll out of my eyes and down my cheeks. "I don't want anyone else. I want you."

He places his hands gently around my face and presses his forehead into mine. "My Riamne," he whispers. I close my eyes against the tears. "I love you always."

The sweet quiet of his aura dissolves, and when I open my eyes, it is as if he was never there. I hold the necklace tightly in my fist, the rough edges of the jewel scratching against my palm. I can feel a thin thread of Calipher's peacefulness coursing through it, stretching up my arm and curling into my chest. It is not enough.

CHAPTER NINE

"Nia? Nia?"

The sun is pushing brightly through the windows. How long have I been standing here?

Tears have crusted at the corners of my eyes. I rub at them with the back of my hand.

"What?"

I force myself back into my surroundings. Bastus stands in front of me. His face is lined with deep concern. "Nia, are you well?"

What a terrible question. How could I be well right now?

"Calipher is gone," I reply.

"I know. That's why I came."

Deep, deep down under the hard outer numbness and the layers of pain underneath it, something stirs inside me. It is kind of him to come, after all that has happened between us.

When I do not respond, he speaks more.

"I am sorry about our fight. It was not fair of me to put all of that on you."

I forgot how angry I was at him. Now that he reminds me, I resent how long it took him to apologize. I resent that he only comes now that Calipher is gone, and he knows there is no one for him to compete with. The resentment hardens in me like coals. But I need him right now. So I just nod.

"Do you know what happened? Why did he leave?"

He pulls his brows together over his blank eyes. "I only know rumors."

"Please. Tell me." The only thing worse than the void Calipher's departure has left in me is how impossible it is to understand.

"It seems Calipher is not the only angel who has...strayed...with humans under their charge." He glances to me. "The rumor is that Theia called them back because she is losing control of them."

All the angels, just gone? I can't get my mind around it.

"Losing control? But—"

"There is more."

He waits for me to look to him.

"People are losing faith in the First Creatures in general, and the gods too. Some are even saying the gods are fighting amongst themselves. That, for the first time, they cannot agree on what to do."

"Is it true? What does Shael say?"

"I cannot hear Him." Bastus fidgets. "Do not share that with anyone. I do not wish to fan the flames."

Calipher is gone, I tell myself. I will myself to believe it, but it will not hold in place. *And everything good has gone with him.*

First Father, then Calipher, and now this? My head spins, and it is as if the very ground below me is slipping away.

"I have to go," I say. "I have loaves to bake."

Bastus blinks back at me. "Do you understand what I just said?"

I stare down at the ground. "I...just...."

I just need to do something. Anything. I need something that I can control.

"What is that in your hand?"

I lift my fist and stare. The necklace is still in it. I pull it close to my chest.

"Calipher gave it to me."

"It has a large amount of magic in it. I can feel it from here."

You will always have a piece of me with you. That is what he said.

"He made it for me."

"I would be careful with that, Nia," he warns. "There is something unusual about it. Would you let me study it, before you do anything with it?"

He stretches a hand out, palm up, and waits. I stare at it. He thinks he can take my necklace from me? The very last thing I have of Calipher? Of course he wants to take it from me...he wanted to take Calipher's place from the beginning.

"No."

I put the necklace around my neck to make the message clear: This is mine, and I am not letting it go. As the chain settles around my neck, it circles me in a soft peace, an echo of Calipher's aura. *All will be well,* it whispers.

Bastus pulls his hand back, and both curl into fists at his sides. His expression is impenetrable. He breathes in, ready to speak, but I cut him off. "Thank you for coming, Bastus. It is time to go."

Then I shut the door on him, before he can say anything else.

CHAPTER TEN

I BAKE LOAF AFTER loaf to keep busy, but it is many days before I can bring myself to go into the village to trade them. I am not sure how many; they begin to bleed together.

It is only when I step out for the walk through the forest that I realize it has not rained—not once, since the terrible storm and my last night with Calipher. The sun is aggressive and moody, glaring down at me. The sky is wide and blank, without any sign of clouds. In town, the ground is so dry dust kicks up with each person's steps, then, without any breeze to carry it, resettles.

The people are sluggish and edgy, a torpid puddle of bodies. The weather is on everyone's minds as clearly as the sweat on their brows.

"Hector said they got rain in the next town a few days ago." I overhear Cyril speaking to Shara as I approach the booths.

Shara shrugs. "And what? Hector says all kinds of things." Her tone is clipped.

"If we can't take it from Hector, then who? He is one of the only ones in this town who trades with anyone outside ourselves."

Cyril's eyes flit toward me and I almost think he sees me, but then they flit back.

"Do not worry about other towns. What good does it do?" she says.

"What good? It shows that what everyone is saying is true. The gods are withholding our rain because of that—" He stops mid-sentence as I approach, and throws his hands out in greeting. "The lovely Nia!"

"Nia, my dear, what have you today?" Shara echoes.

I look down to my empty hands and realize my basket is still at home.

"My regrets, I am not making trades. Not today."

"Oh, but such a lovely woman should not be empty-handed!" Cyril exclaims.

Shara rolls her eyes and turns away to draw in more profitable customers.

I turn to leave, but Cyril rushes out from his booth to my side.

"Please, my dear," he says, gesturing grandly as he holds out apples for me to take. "A gift."

"No, no, I have nothing to trade for it today. I will bring you loaves of bread tomorrow, and then I will trade with you."

"Allow me to give you this modest gift. All I ask in return is a smile from the beautiful Nia."

A choked laugh escapes me. I am so surprised I don't know what to say. Cyril has always been kind, but this is not kindness. His words scrawl uncomfortably under my skin, making me want to pull away.

"Please!" he pleads. "Do not turn away my gift! I could bear anything but that."

"Oh..."

He sees my hesitation, and he actually looks hurt. He presses again, his voice raising, and he kneels in front of me. A few other villagers glance our way, giving me a dirty look. His wife is just feet away, just returned to their booth.

Cyril worships his wife.

"Fine, fine." I grab the fruits from his outstretched hands. "Are you feeling quite well, Cyril?"

"Always, when you are near. Better than well. Wonderful!"

"Well...I have to go. Go back to your booth." I pull away from him. "With your wife."

I do not know where I will go from here, but Cyril's attention is unnerving. He is not himself. Perhaps it is the heat—it has taken a toll on us all.

"Nia!"

I turn toward another voice, confused. It is not Cyril this time, thank the gods, but who else would bother? The market is a place where people come to mingle, but not with me. Especially lately, with the rumors they have been passing about Calipher and me.

I realize with a strange wave of feeling that there was a time when I would have given anything for this attention, and not so long ago. But I am not that girl anymore, and my soul is raw and tender in Calipher's wake. It is all I can bear to be alone right now. Coming into the village was a mistake. I am not ready for this yet.

A young man with golden-brown hair waves at me. It is Ferris, a boy I played with as a young child. We have hardly spoken in years. He pushes right through the others to get to me.

"Ferris?" He closes the last few feet between us and wraps his arms around me, fruits and all. "Ferris, what's wrong?"

"What is wrong is that I love you, and I've only just realized it," he says. "You must be mine."

I am so shocked that a single bubble of laughter bursts from me.

"Why are you laughing?" he growls. "I said that I love you."

His hand closes around my wrist, and it pinches.

I study his face. His eyes are wide and unfocused, tense around the edges, as if something urgent has happened.

But he cannot be serious. He hardly remembers I live here, most of the time.

"I do not understand—"

"You must be mine," he presses. "You must. I cannot bear to be without you even one more turn of the sun."

I try to pull away from his firm grip. He clings to me desperately, without reason.

This must be some sort of cruel joke. I know the village has been wary of my involvement with a First Creature, but this is too far.

"Ferris, stop this."

"How can you expect me to stop, just as I have discovered how desperately I need you?"

His eyes are dilated so wide the bright blue of his irises are but a thin ring about a sea of black. They quiver at the edges, strange and unsteady. An uneasy buzz rises in my ears and my gut twists. If this is a gag, some way to shame me for my actions, it has gone too far.

Finally I break free of him, and I run, dropping apples in my wake. Or the closest to running that I can manage while weaving through the midday market crowd.

As I push my way through, more voices call my name, more hands reach out to grab me. At one point, a man lunges in front of another to get close to me, and the second man pulls him back and punches him in the face. I do not stop running until the forest trees hide me from the village and I am sure I am alone.

My heart won't stop racing. I knew that the village had turned wary of me, but I have never known my neighbors to be so cruel. Suddenly, it all catches up with me, and I burst into tears.

"What is wrong?"

I jump to hear another man's voice behind me, but when I see it is only Bastus, I am so grateful there are no words for it. I fling my arms around him.

"It was so strange," I manage between sobs. "I have known these people all my life. I never known them to be so cruel. It was like they were possessed."

He tightens his arms around me protectively, and guilt washes over me. I push away from him and stutter out an explanation of the strange behavior of the villagers in the market, neighbors I have known most of my life.

"And the look in their eyes. Like the person I've always know them to be was replaced by something else." I shudder.

Bastus leans toward me, his shoulders pulled in and tense. "All of them, they had the same expression?"

I pause to think. "Cyril and Ferris, yes. I am not sure of the others. I was too surprised. It did not make any sense."

Bastus shakes his head. "I warned you," he mutters.

"What do you mean?"

He sighs and looks at me reproachfully. "It is the necklace, Nia."

"Calipher's necklace?" I instinctively wrap my hand around the chain that dangles from my neck. It is hard to say his name. "What could any of this have to do with the necklace?

"I told you, it's drenched in magic," he says. "Whatever Calipher did to it, it is affecting the people around you. Did Calipher say anything when he gave it to you?"

"He said...." I sigh. I don't want to think about that. Not ever, but especially now, when I am so upset already. "He said Theia was calling him to the Host and he would not be coming back this time. That he wanted me to always be loved by someone the way he loved me. That this was a way I could always have a piece of him with me."

Bastus' whole body goes rigid. "Nia, take the necklace off."

"No!" I pull away, even though he has made no gesture toward me.

"Do you not get it? He charmed it with some kind of love spell. Let me have it, and I will destroy it for you."

He stretches out his palm and waits.

I stare down at it, the necklace gripped so tightly in my palm its rough corners dig into my skin. Inside my chest, I can feel it resisting, knotting around my heart and taking root.

"It is mine." It is all I can think to say. It is mine, it is the last of Calipher I have, and I am keeping it.

"You must, Nia. It is the only way. This is no joke. If you go on wearing it, what just happened in the village is only the beginning."

For a brief pause, I waver. A quiver of fear runs through me. But then a hot surge of anger bursts over it, and I am all sparks and licking flames. *How dare Bastus tell me what to do, as if I am some helpless child still?*

"Worse? From a love charm? Please," I sneer. "You are only jealous that I cling to what Calipher left me, instead of running to you."

His face crumples in a way I have never seen before—somewhere between injured and outraged.

"Jealous!" he cries. "Of what? Of loving his own Will so much he had to be called back by his goddess?"

His expression wrings at my heart. I almost wrap my arms around him, I almost apologize and beg him to forgive me—explain that I don't understand what is wrong with me lately, but I want to set it right again.

But then something else stirs inside me. It is more than anger, more than grief. *So he is mad? Good. Let him be mad.*

"You have to listen to me, Nia. Everything is going wrong right now. Even the humans can feel it—can't you? Magic can interfere—just like what you have around your neck. It can make things worse. It is dangerous.

"I am not sure what he has done, but it is like he used his angel's magic to cast a charm that belongs to Gloros. I do not think he meant for all this to happen, but something went very wrong. The gods' magic is not for us to mix.

"Just let me—"

He reaches toward me—toward *it*—as he speaks.

"No!"

It bursts from me in a wild shriek, a sound I did not even know I could make. At the same time, my arm swings wildly in front of me, casting him backward.

As he stumbles backward, trying to regain balance, his eyes are wide and startled, reflecting back my own surprise at what I have done. I did not know I had such strength in me. Did I even touch him?

Does it matter? the voice inside me prompts. It is what he deserves, if he is going to interfere.

"No, Bastus. Calipher gave it to me."

Calipher's warm peacefulness pulses out of the necklace and floods my chest.

All expression fades from Bastus' face until it is completely blank.

"Nia. Calm down. You have to understand—"

"I do not."

He bites his lip. His arms move out to his sides, his hands stretching out as if cautiously approach a wild animal.

"Magic like what you have dangling around your neck right now...it is not a decoration. It is not a toy. And it is not meant for humans."

I am fed up with everyone treating me like I need protection. Like I am made of glass.

"Calipher would not give me something dangerous," I retort. "I think I can handle a necklace."

"Look Nia. I know it is hard for you to understand, but there is something wrong with Calipher. He hasn't been himself for a long time."

"Are you saying I broke him?"

"No! Nia...." Bastus takes a deep breath and looks back to me. "Actually, yes. It is not your fault. But yes, when Calipher chose you over Theia, it broke him."

"That is impossible." My voice is raw and my cheeks grow wet with tears.

"The magic that holds the realms in order is complex and subtle, and when set out of order, dangerous. Right now, everything is very, very out of order."

I don't know what to say. For a moment we both just stand there, me sniffling, him staring at the ceiling above my head.

"Nia, I know it does not feel right, right now. I know it is working inside you to protect itself. I can see it working at you."

He takes a slow step forward, his arms still outstretched.

"I need you to trust me. I am not doing this out of jealousy. Or anger. Or hate. I do this for you, Nia. I do this from love. I know you do not see it right now, but you will. Give me the necklace."

An anger bursts from my core like a firestorm. It burns away everything else like a purge.

"No."

What happens next unfolds too quickly for me to understand. In a rush of smoke, Bastus closes the space between us and grabs the necklace, trying to steal it away from me. Just as quickly, there is a bright flash, and Bastus is thrust away again and crashes into a tree.

For a breath, he just sits there where he landed. "Gods, Calipher, what were you thinking?"

I stand there and wait, my head buzzing, my fingers trembling—is it from the power I feel pulsing through me or fear?

When Bastus stands up and looks at me, I expect him to yell back, to mirror my rage. But instead, he steps away, toward the door. His blank eyes look me over with what feels like sadness.

"I'm here when you're ready, Nia."

And then he turns and walks away.

A swirl of guilt and shame wrestle through me—this is Bastus, my truest friend. And I just drove him away. I want to run after him. I want him to soothe me and tell me it will be all right, to hold my hands in his until they stop shaking.

But then the feeling rushes over me again, an echo of Calipher's presence that swirls inside me and promises me it will be all right.

I stay put, and watch Bastus disappear into the woods.

Chapter Eleven

I ONLY TRY TO go to market one more time. That is enough for me to stop.

The men keep rushing to me, and a few women too, grabbing at me. It is worse than the last time. They crowd around me, fight to reach me, and I can hardly move around among them. I am a little more prepared this time, and I manage to complete my shopping, but Shara and the traders don't seem pleased at the mess I bring to their doors. At least, the ones who are not after me. This time I know it can't possibly be a joke.

Eventually a fight broke out. The hit was like cracking glass, breaking something in the tension, and everything blew to pieces.

I ran. And I will not go back.

Just when I believe I am safe and out of sight from the village, a hand grabs my arm. Ferris saw me as I tried to slip away down the path, and insists on making sure I get home safely—as if there is anything out here to harm me, besides him.

He stays on my tail the entire way to my door. When I open it, he shifts as if to follow me in when I open the door. I have to pull it quickly behind me and lock it to keep him out.

He does not turn back to town after I shut him out. He stands there in the yard the rest of the day, in the unforgiving heat. He is still there when Mother comes home.

"What is Ferris up to out there?"

I don't know how to explain to her without it starting a fight, and I can't bear another fight right now. Not after this day.

"I do not know. I already asked him if he needs something. He does not. Let us just ignore him, please, and have our dinner."

Mother stares at me a little too long, with that careful, scrutinizing way of hers. I stare back, hoping the uneasiness I feel does not show in my eyes.

The meal is not my best. I had to leave the market without all the spices I needed for it. But Mother does not seem to notice. She keeps one eye on the window all evening, and on Ferris pacing back and forth past it.

The next day is punishingly hot. The sun beats its way into the house, even with the curtains drawn. Ferris is still out there when I wake, and he doesn't budge all day. I consider putting out some water for him, but that would be like feeding a stray cat; it would only keep him here longer. Eventually he will grow too thirsty, and he will go home, and things will settle back to their normal ways again.

He has to.

I do not dare go into the village again. I decide to wait a few days until things have calmed down. Then everything will go back to normal, and the town will forget.

By nightfall, a few more admirers have joined Ferris outside in the yard—Dorian, who used to be a hand on Mother's fields before he started his own, and Jerome, a boy I used to help watch when he was younger. They both stand there restless and tense, the same blank hungry stare on their faces as Ferris. When I pass the window, they call out and run for me, so I learn to duck when I go past them. I begin to feel like a hostage in my own home.

But if I ignore them, they will go away. Surely.

The heat does not let up. It only becomes muggier, the thick air making it harder to breathe. Mother comes home hungry and cranky from a rough day in the fields, and the villagers collecting outside her home do nothing to lift her mood.

"It is Calipher," I stutter, grasping for something to explain them. The sound of his name causes the emerald to flutter waves of his aura through me. "They are convinced he will return, and that when he does, he will come here."

It is partially true.

Mother grumbles, but she leaves it at that. She takes her second-day stew and falls asleep in her chair shortly after, too exhausted from a long day of fighting the heat to question it.

We are going to run out of food soon. I have to find a way to get rid of these men.

It is mid-morning of the third day when Ferris finally collapses from the heat.

I only realize it when the growing crowd starts to grumble and shout.

When I peek out the window, Ferris is on the ground unconscious and some of the others are kicking at him, hard. And they are laughing.

I panic—these are not men anymore, these are monsters.

I race out before I know what I am doing, and then realize I am helpless to stop it—what can I do against an angry, dazed mob?

I kick at the dust and it cakes to my face, beads of sweat already forming under the sun's glare. Blood covers Ferris' face, though I cannot tell where it is coming from.

The anger and fear simmers up in me and I shout at them, "Get away! Stop it!" A helpless plea that comes out in a shrill, shaky tone I have never heard from my own throat before.

But they stop immediately. They turn away from Ferris and look to me.

I run to him without thinking.

He is limp and unconscious, welts and bruises already forming across his face, and also his arms and legs. My heart pounds in distress.

"Jerome, water."

He does it. He grabs the jug we keep in the house and runs back to us. I try to tilt some water into Ferris, but it splatters all around, and I cannot tell if it is working or not. He remains unconscious. The others leer around me, a garble of desperate pleas for my affections and grumbles about finishing the boy. I cannot leave him here. But I do not dare bring him into the house, and oh gods, I do not have the strength to take him back to the village.

Not by myself, at least.

I stand abruptly, knocking into some as they hover over us, a thought growing in my mind. But will it work? The warm pulse of the necklace tells me it is right.

"Carry Ferris to his home. Do not harm him," I order.

The men rush around, eager to be the first to follow my command. When they have gathered and lifted Ferris carefully from the ground, I smile and nod. I can see in their hungry blank eyes that this is reward enough for them.

"Very good. Now go."

As I watch the men disappear into the woods, an aura of sweet relief and satisfaction fills me to the brim. They are gone. With this weight from my shoulders, I feel free to grieve the loss of Calipher in peace for the first time since he left. I sigh, tilt my head back to the sun—so like Calipher's own golden hair—and let it fill me. It feels bottomless, all-consuming.

But it is a relief to simply feel it, finally.

"They will all be back again, you know."

I spin around toward the voice. It is Bastus, of course.

Guilt puddles in my chest, spoiling my moment of indulgence, and I resent him for it. He is so persistent, always an opinion ready about what I should do, who I should be with. As if his feelings for me give him the right to tell me what to do, when really all he's done is break our friendship.

"What happened?" he asks. His voice is soft, but his expression is hard.

But why should I feel guilty? I did not do anything to Ferris. I stopped it—I *saved* him.

"He collapsed from the heat, and the others...I didn't see it at first."

Bastus rolls his lips into a thin line and shuts his eyes against me.

"These men, they—" I stutter over my words, searching for the right ones to explain.

He cuts me off. "You know it is not them, Nia. Take the necklace off."

The way he looks at me. He looks wounded. No—disappointed, most deeply. The necklace throbs through me with waves of sweet quiet, shielding me from him. *You will not stand here and be chastised like a child.*

I straighten up and hold my head high. "Thank you for coming by, Bastus. But it was not necessary."

And then I turn away and walk back into the house, my mind crowding with anxieties.

Is Bastus right? Is it my fault?

My fingers drift to the necklace and wrap around it. Calipher made me this necklace. The shadow of his presence, that intoxicating peaceful aura, pulses through me, and it is enough.

Chapter Twelve

Ferris is back again the very next day, his face black and swollen, his pacing now clipped with a limp. The others return, too.

They all seem to be tolerating each other peacefully enough for now, but the heat continues to mount, and so does their restlessness. They pace between the house and the woods endlessly.

Exhaustion from long days in the fields in the hot sun has kept my mother from investigating it too carefully so far. But it will not last. And then what will I say? How long will they keep it up? The questions torture me for days.

The herd outside our house is sluggish and weary, but they keep it up anyway. Instead of shrinking as admirers give up and go home, it grows. Half the village must be out there by now. I have not left this heat trap of a house for just as long, not since Ferris collapsed.

We're running out of food.

So they continue to pace outside my house, and I pace within it. I have to do something.

They listened to me when I commanded them before, so maybe they will listen to me again. It's been rolling through my mind ever since the last time, but I have been afraid to leave the house.

I take a deep breath and wrap my hand around the emerald to collect my nerves. Then I storm out the door.

"Boys." Some of them are older than my mother. But 'boys' feels right. As if I am the one in charge. "Come here."

They stop their pacing and perk up at my voice. And then they listen—they come to me, all of them.

Thank the gods.

No, thank the necklace.

They watch me with intent. With adoration. The way Calipher used to. It satisfies something buried deep within me that I did not even know was there.

It gives me the courage to keep going.

"Go away."

I try to muster the authority and urgency of last time, when I ordered them to take Ferris home. Despite the uncertainty that shakes my chest, I think I succeed.

But they do not turn to leave. The adoration on their faces darkens into frowns. They grumble and murmur.

"No, my lady." I cannot see who the voice comes from, somewhere near the back. "I will never leave, my love."

"Nor I!"

"Never!"

A cacophony of resistance rises. I step back, toward the house.

"You must! This cannot go on!" Already the strength in my voice is faltering.

"I pledge my love to Nia, and I will never leave her."

They are restless and uneasy like a storm cloud, thick and electric and about to burst. But they listened to me before. They listened to me now, until I tried to send them away. What is different?

"Please, Nia, be mine. I cannot bear to be without you." One of them steps forward and tries to take my hand. I jump back to get away.

Another edges closer, boxing out the first. It hardly matters which is which anymore; they are an endless mob of the same blank stare.

I edge back a little more. *Think*, I command myself. *Think.* Something is different. I just wish I knew what.

"Why! Why will you not do as I command!" I stomp the ground in helpless rage.

"I will do anything my love commands!" one cries, reaching for my hand. I pull back again. "My Nia, just tell me what would please you."

It hits me like a lightning bolt. Last time I asked them *to* do something. Now I am asking them *not* to do something.

It is worth trying.

I straighten up and try to feel commanding.

"I command you: Go to your homes. Eat your dinners. Drink from your jugs. Love your families. Rest."

For a dead pause that sends a chill down my spine, they stare at me with those haunting blank expressions. And then they turn and trail back toward the village. Every last one of them.

They will be back, I am sure of it. But for now, they are gone.

Once they have enough of a lead, I run to get my basket and head into the village myself.

As I make my trades and stock up on the foods we will need, it dawns on me: It's almost all women. Women trading, women vending, women's crops available for trade. I could not bear to study the admirers lurking outside my home carefully, but now I realize that more than half the villagers must be under the necklace's pull. Those left uncharmed cast dark glares my way, and I can hear their murmurs to each other—the judgments and assumptions, the rumors.

They say the gods punished my family once for meddling with things we should not, and that They will do it again.

The mention of my father burns, and it pains me to consider what he might think of me now. Shame simmers all the way down into my fingertips, but I wrap a hand around the emerald and remember that Calipher is with me. It soothes me with its aura, curling up inside me and numbing the anger away.

Each time a stray new man comes at me pledging his love, I order him home.

A pulse of warmth flows into me from the necklace, filling me with Calipher's aura. Under the rush of pleasure it gives me, there is a bittersweet pang, like a homesickness.

But I get what I need from the village without further trouble, and return home. When Mother comes home her eyes flit immediately out the window to the front of the house. When she finds it empty, her mood shifts. She takes her seat, I place a full hot meal before her, and we have a pleasant, quiet evening for once.

See? Bastus was wrong, the necklace whispers to me. Everything is under control. We are in control.

I am so filled with its peaceful presence that it prickles along my neck. Finally, all is well.

Chapter Thirteen

The admirers begin to recollect outside our home again the next day.

I stare at them from the window, my hair sticking to the sweat that gathers along my brow and neck. How are there not any clouds? How long can this unbearable heat keep up?

Along with the heat, a shaky disquiet mounts inside me. But the necklace pulses its aura over me, and my anxieties wash away.

It assures me the admirers are of no consequence. Not now that I know how to deal with them. I will let them gather throughout the day, and send them all home again at once before Mother comes home.

For now, I let the necklace drown out the anxiety with more pleasant feelings as I complete my other chores. I have not felt this good since the day Calipher took me up on the mountain, by the river, and the full power of his aura came over me for the first time as we pressed into each other. It floats me through the rest of the day.

Until the back door slams open abruptly mid-afternoon, jolting me back to myself. My mother storms in, a wobbly mess.

"You're early!" I scramble to my feet.

The admirers are still out front. I inch over to block her view out the window, my mind scrambling for an excuse to go out front so I can order them away.

"Such heat," she replies, slumping into her chair.

I bring her water. She takes it wordlessly, a terrible scowl on her face. I stare out the window and watch the men. If only I could will them away from inside the house. I have never once seen my mother leave the fields early before. Her mood has spoiled like milk, out in that piercing heat.

As she drinks and rests, my mind races—I must find an excuse to go out front. One that will not draw her attention to what is out there. But my thoughts are blank.

What does it matter? the necklace urges. What is she to us?

But she is something, is she not? She is my mother. And yet, what has she ever done for you? Scolded and ignored and held you back.

I am grasping for an answer when Mother speaks.

"What are you staring at?"

She stands and turns toward the window, and a black dread swallows my heart.

"Back again!" she snarls. Her hands ball into fists and her temper ignites behind her eyes. "Enough!"

"Mother, wait—"

I reach for her, but she is already past me and to the door. I fly to the window, too afraid to be near mother when she realizes all these admirers are here for me. She flings the door open and storms outside.

"Enough is enough!" she growls. "Cyril! Ferris! All of you! Leave!"

"I will never leave," Cyril declares. "Not while this is where my Nia resides."

The others join in with rumblings of agreement. My heartbeat rushes into my ears, and the windowsill creaks under the pressure of my tightening grip.

"Nia?" Mother blinks at them. "You are here for *Nia*? Come off it," Mother says with a hard, short laugh.

"No one laughs at my Nia," Cyril declares. His face no longer holds the slack blankness it did before. Now his heavy brows are folded forward in rage, and his jaw clenched, teeth bared.

He rushes forward and shoves mother backwards, and her head crashes into my window so hard the glass cracks. I jump away with a gasp.

The others swell to Cyril's sides, surrounding Mother. Their expressions are similarly dark.

Mother gathers herself, pushing away from the house. "I speak of my daughter any way I choose. But you have no claim to her, or the land you stand on," Mother snaps back. "Leave. Now."

What happens next is so overwhelming, so strange, so terrible, I cannot believe my senses. Through the window I see Cyril's expression harden. I am gripped by fear and think to run out to Mother, to order them away, but before I can a powerful pulse from the necklace overcomes me, and I do not.

A twitch at the edge of his mouth, and then Cyril's arm rushes forward and slams Mother flying backwards again, but this time there is no space behind her to stumble through. She slams back against the house with a terrible crack, and her head slams through the window. I duck just in time to avoid the flying glass, and a scream escapes me.

"Step back! Leave her alone!"

They do as I command. I eye Cyril and the others a moment before daring to go out to check Mother's wounds.

I kneel to her side and call to her, but her body is limp and her eyes stare blankly at nothing.

Heat rushes to my face as if I were drowning in it, and suddenly everything around me feels very, very far away.

"Go away!" I shriek into the house wall. I whip around at Cyril. "Go! Go home!"

As I sink into hysterical sobs, one by one they trail off toward their homes.

CHAPTER
FOURTEEN

"RIAMNE."

It is Bastus. Who else?

I am not sure how much time has passed, or how long he has been standing there, but it is dark now.

I slipped away to somewhere else, sitting here with my mother's body. I have stared at her grimaced face so long that my shock has given way to numbness.

I thought I was in control, that I could keep the admirers in order. But it all happened in a blink, before I could even see she was in any real danger.

Bastus places a hand on my shoulder and I take in the restless eagerness that swims through him.

When he speaks, his voice is gentle, as if to swathe me up like a small child. "Would you like me to send her off to Shael at the river for you? Or we could...." he clears his throat. "We could bury her, if you like."

My heart swells. It is kind of him to offer to perform Theia's rites for me, in the absence of an angel to do it. But it would only make my heart ache for Calipher.

"No. If she considered herself a follower of anyone, it was Gloros. We should burn her."

My voice sounds calm and in control. As if it belongs to someone else.

"Then that is what we will do," he says.

He is being so good to me—better than I deserve. But I know what is coming. Eventually he will come back to the necklace again.

And what has it done for me, really? Where has it gotten me? My need to keep Calipher close has taken away the last of my family. The necklace. My hand is wrapped around it now. What did it do to me, in that moment before it happened? As if it knew...but that is impossible.

I listen for the nudging voice inside me, but it has fallen silent.

"I'll send for Peri." Bastus dissolves into shadow and darts off into the village.

While I wait I sit next to my mother and study her wounds. It was brutal and vicious, what Cyril did to her. The necklace, the heat, the village's growing tensions. Perhaps something like this was inevitable.

Peri is just on Bastus' tail, soaring low through the air.

I stand. Without words, we form a small audience around my mother's body.

"Nia, I'm so sorry," she says.

I don't know what to say. I nod instead. How much did Bastus tell her about what happened? Does she know about the necklace?

"Would you like to do a prayer over her together?" she asks.

I stare down at her stiffening body.

"No. Let's just burn her."

"Already? Are you sure? Would you not like to wait and have the village?"

The village? The ones who have shut us out for so long, and blamed us for their misfortunes? The ones who stalked me for so many days and brought this terrible event upon me?

"No."

Peri nods. With some orchestration of her hands, she begins to draw out branches and sticks from the woods. They float to us and shape themselves into a sort of altar. Then she turns and gestures toward my mother's body, and it rises off the ground and floats on top of it.

Bastus and I follow her lead, and she stands across the altar from us, pronouncing Gloros' death ritual over my mother.

"Dust to dust, flame to flame, dream to dream," she begins. "It is the way of all things, and now it is the way of this one, Lina, farmer, wife, mother, a woman of great passions and great dreams, as are we all...."

For followers of Gloros, it always comes back to passions. They are chasers of dreams, pursuers of great emotions, valuing them all equally, the good and the bad.

Was my mother a woman of passions? I realize I do not know. I always thought of her as a woman of great burdens. A woman of duty. A woman who wanted her dinner hot and her home quiet.

It is *my* passions that have landed us here.

As Peri speaks, she casts charms to pull more tinder from the forest and sets it around the body for the end. When it is big enough she snaps her fingers, and the tinder catches fire.

"And now we give Lina back to the realm, and the goddess who loves her. May her soul carry on into the next with passion bright enough to light the darkest nights, on through the end of time."

Then we stand there and watch my mother break apart and drift away in ashes. By the time it is finished, the first hints of day are starting to show from the east.

Before Peri leaves, she places a kind hand on my shoulder. "Feel your grief, Nia. And whatever else comes with it. Listen to what it has to say. If you try to escape it, it will keep growing until it consumes you."

She gives me a half-hearted smile of comfort, and squeezes my shoulder. Then she flies away. Suddenly it hits me how exhausted I am. I drop to the ground and sit. Bastus paces nearby.

"Go ahead. Get it over with," I say.

"Nia, come on."

"No. I know you have something to get off your chest. So do it."

"Your mother just died, you should...." He stops pacing, his back to me. He stares at the ground, caught in reflection. "You are right. I do have things to say. Grief or not, you need to hear them. It might as well be now."

He turns around and stands in front of me.

"Nia, I don't know what has had you spiraling out of control, but it has got to stop. Everything is falling apart. *You* are falling apart, whether you realize it or not."

"So you are going to blame me, too? I do not control the rain!"

"No—no. But Nia...tensions are high, and you are adding coals to the fire." He leans forward so that he is looking into my eyes. "Are you hearing me, Nia? Are you understanding?"

His blank, earnest gaze is too much. I look away and stare into the forest instead.

"When Theia called the angels back, it set waves throughout Terath. The other creatures are angry. Saying She had no right. That the First Creatures are owed their own will, just like the humans. Some are even saying they would fight for it. There are even rumors of a few angels who were already so far gone they were able to resist Theia's summons. Do you know how dangerous that is? Disconnected angels drifting through Terath?"

He pauses and waits for me. But I have nothing to say.

"It if is true, then a war between the realms is coming. In some ways, it has already begun. Even men are murmuring of ending the gods' reign. Everything is swaying off kilter. The rain, the heat, this is only the beginning, Terath is—"

His rant comes to an abrupt halt. I realize suddenly that tears are streaming twin rivers down my face.

"I'm sorry," he whispers. "I hate being at odds with you. We must stop this."

A pang of sadness strikes through me like a lightning bolt. "What do you want from me, Bastus?"

He reaches out and takes my hand, folds it between his own. Finally he is looking at me, really seeing me again.

"The necklace. Take it off."

No. The voice inside me that responds is vicious and stubborn.

But it is not mine.

I do not want to take it off, either. It is the only thing I have left of Calipher. The only way I have to hold onto this peacefulness I have come to need—and I do need it, now more than ever.

But if I am honest with myself, the necklace is beginning to frighten me. A person is dead—my *mother* is dead. Whether Calipher meant for the necklace to have so much power or not, this has gone too far.

That woman never cared for you anyway. Not since your father passed. Do not let her spoil the rest for you.

I run my fingers over the chain and lift it. As I do, I can feel it pulling against me, begging to stay. The warmth it filled me with dredges through me and turns to rough, grinding edges.

Bastus shakes his head. "It's not your fault, Nia. Calipher made his own choices. And even if he had made the right choices, the others were still out there. But I'm scared. Everything is wrong. The entire realm. You have the power to help make it a little better."

I take a deep breath, and pull the necklace off in a quick motion. I ball up the chain in my fist and look up to Bastus. He kisses my forehead.

"Your father would be proud," he says.

I do not know if this is true, but I appreciate the gesture. I turn away and place the necklace into my jewelry box, then set it up on a high shelf in the kitchen.

"I miss him." I try to form the words but what comes out is more of a sob.

"I know," he replies. He opens his arms and I lean forward into his chest. His large, strong arms fold around me like a shield from the world, and his eager restlessness fills me.

My arms wrap tight around him, and his restless aura begins to wake up my mind. It is strange, how solid he feels, even though this form he lives in is not his true one. He chooses to look so like men that I forget sometimes how very different Bastus is from me. He is not a man at all. He is a First Creature. A demon.

A shape shifter.

A thought rushes to the forefront of my mind. An unsettled feeling in my stomach tells me to shove it aside, but the idea of it feels too good to let go of. The only thing that feels good right now at all. Taking the necklace off has left me hollow and achy, and I need to feel something else right now. Anything else.

"Bastus?"

"Yes?"

"Can you take *any* shape?"

His muscles flex in a wave against me. We never speak of what he is. Not like this.

"Yes."

I pull away so I can watch his face. "You can look like someone else? Someone who is gone?"

He hesitates, his brows pulling together into a frown as he starts to understand. "I can...but, Nia...." He shakes his head, out of words.

"Please. Just this once. Just let me look at him."

A slow, heavy sigh eases from him. But then he lets go of me and stands. "Just this once. And only for you."

Only for me. He would do anything for me, I know this. Guilt twists in my stomach—it is why I asked. I knew he would, for me.

He steps back, then breaks apart into dark shadow, a whirling torrent. Then the shadow comes back together in a new form. My father.

"There now," my father's form says. He stretches his arms out to me.

Hot shame floods my cheeks. It is good—and strange—to see my father again after so many years. I run my eyes over his form and take in all the details, those little things about him my child's mind was not able to hold onto—the way his eyes crinkled at the edges, the way his grin was a little crooked.

But he misunderstood. I shake my head.

"Not him." I mutter it into my chest, too embarrassed to look him in the eye. Too afraid of the expression that I know will break over his face when he understands.

A stiff tension builds between us. And then the rustle of whirling shadow returns.

This time, when he takes shape, he is Calipher.

It is strange, seeing Calipher and feeling Bastus' aura tingling under my skin. Like leaning into a rose and smelling a lilac. But it is such a great relief to see him again. Like coming home. Bastus chose to take his form with silver wings, like he was when I first reached out to touch them. A sweet detail that does not go unnoticed. A reminder of better times.

Calipher-Bastus comes forward to close the space between us and wraps his arms around me again. His skin has the same feel of cool marble. It's all exactly the same.

Except for his eyes. When I look into his eyes, they aren't the soft silver like Calipher has. They are blank. As if there is nothing behind them. I choose to ignore this, because I need to. My head is woozy with all that has happened, and my heart is weak. I need his comfort, even if it comes like this.

Before I realize what I am doing, I lean in and kiss him. His lips melt into mine, but then he flinches away.

"Not like this, Nia," he whispers. "Please."

He is right. This is wrong. He deserves better.

I almost pull away. But I miss him so terribly.

When I kiss him again, his guard breaks down. He hesitates, then kisses me back. A long, soft kiss packed with all his desire, all his years of longing and loneliness. The next thing I know, we are sprawled out on the dusty, thirsty ground, our robes pooled around us.

It is different this time, and not just because of the strange buzz of his mismatched aura. Where Calipher was primal and urgent, Bastus is gentle and warm.

With my eyes closed and Bastus' aura pulsing over me, I can't hold on to Calipher's presence. So I keep my eyes open and watch as the morning sun rises, glistening off of his wings, spread wide around us.

It is not enough, but it is as close as I can get. It lessens the void inside me that the necklace left behind.

The restless heat works between us. The thick air clings to our skin. As the sun tips over the horizon, it sticks to us in lazy, hot beams.

When we are done, he rolls away from me, sitting up and curling into himself. His expression is gloomy and stiff.

Suddenly I feel as though he is realms apart from me. As if we have been severed forever in some way.

"Bastus, I—"

"Yesterday was a terrible day for you." He cuts me off. "You should be in bed."

His voice is gentle, but he won't look at me. Still in Calipher's form, he wraps my robe around me, scoops me into his arms, and carries me into the house.

He places me in my bed. "Now rest."

"Bastus."

He still won't look at me. Instead he leans over me and kisses my forehead.

"Bastus. Don't leave like this. You're worrying me."

He turns away.

"You will come see me later?" I beg.

He squeezes my hand, and then Calipher's form breaks away into shadow, and both of them are gone, leaving me all alone.

CHAPTER FIFTEEN

IN THE DAYS AFTER my mother's death, I keep finding myself outside the house, staring at the sky. I wait for the rain to come back. If the gods were withholding it from us because of my sins with Calipher, because of my sins coveting his gift, haven't I suffered enough to pay for it yet? Haven't the people in the village? The poor thirsty crops of my fields?

I took the necklace off.

But still the rain doesn't come. Each day the buzz of the air's flat heat builds. The ground has crumbled to dust that kicks up in the wind and stings the eyes. The sun beats so strongly my shoulders sag under it. All the wheat of my mother's fields, already a sickly yellow, begins to wilt back toward the earth.

My body feels stale and crusted in guilt. My head throbs with grief. The air is heavy with the moisture that will not drop to the ground, making me work to pull it in and out of my lungs.

I should do something.

Usually, a murder like my mother's is something to report to the village council. But what could I say to them? How to explain?

And if I do not, how do I explain Mother's death then? She is still gone, either way.

In my sadness and shock, no action feels appropriate. So I drift through the sweltering days the best I can, and let the others spread the word that Lina has passed away. Let the rumors spread.

Around me, the town is slowly going mad, folding under the sun's pressure. Fights break out over nothing at the market. The people are so out of control that when I go back home sometimes I climb up on top of the cupboard to make sure the necklace is still there, safely hidden away—that I have not, in my desperate emptiness, slipped it back around my neck.

Without Mother's presence looming over the house, I find a new kind of quiet in it. There is no one to bluster in at the end of the day, none of her stormy moods souring the space. No one to snap and grumble, or to sit in a silent haze in the corner as if I do not exist at all.

Within the home, it is as if the clouds have cleared, and let the sunshine through.

No, I chide myself. I miss her. I do. She did not deserve the end she got.

And this is true. But so is all the rest of it.

With her gone, what about the fields? How will I keep trading for food once the existing grain is gone? The questions fester, always at the back of my mind, but no answers come to me.

I am shocked out of my thoughts by a rap at the door. No one has made their way out this far since Mother died and I took the necklace off.

When I open the door, I find myself face to face with Cyril, coated in sweat and panting, clearly struggling from the walk out here and the heat. A wave of anger and fear wash over me. My hand wanders compulsively to my throat, checking for the necklace that is not there.

"What are you doing here?"

But this is not the Cyril the necklace had a hold on, the mindless follower who slammed Mother back against the house. This Cyril has dark circles under his eyes, and his skin is sallow. He keeps pushing his hair back from his forehead, as if it were keeping him from seeing something gravely important.

"Your mother," he says. He speaks so quickly the words run together. "I couldn't have, could I? I wouldn't. Nia, you must tell me it is not true. I keep seeing it over and over."

The strange way his bloodshot eyes wander makes the back of my neck prickle with uneasiness.

"Cyril, calm down. What are you trying to say?"

"It is crazy, I know it is," he says. "But I need you to tell me, Nia. Tell me I did not kill Lina."

I open my mouth to speak, then close it again, at a loss for words. What does he remember? His eyes flicker over my face.

"Oh gods, oh gods, oh gods...." He says it to himself more than to me. "It was real, it was real."

What can I say to explain? I reach out and place a hand on his shoulder. He reads my face.

"I hoped it was a dream. It has to have been. Why would I hurt Lina? It all felt so far away and removed. But it felt so necessary. It felt...it felt...." He squints, losing his words in thoughts. "You. I had to do it for you...."

A sickening darkness wrenches through my core. It didn't occur to me that he might remember.

"Cyril." I shake him by his shoulder to pull his attention back to me. His eyes roll reluctantly to mine. "What happened...it was not your fault."

I am not sure where I am going with this. I just need him to be calm.

"But I killed her. I killed Lina. The wife of one my greatest friends, and a good business partner."

"No, Cyril." My hand is a fist, clenched tight around his robe. "What you remember, it was not you."

I need him to let this go. It is the only way I can let it go. But how can I make him understand without explaining it all to him?

He blinks. "But...."

"You were under a magical influence."

"Magic?" He looks dazed.

"Yes."

"But we have to tell. What if it happens again?" He looks at me the way a child looks to a parent. Like he is lost, like he needs someone else's direction.

"It won't. The magic that made it happen is gone."

"Gone?"

"Yes. It is gone."

He nods, but his eyes are empty, and I know he still does not understand.

"I killed her, Nia. How could I do that?"

"No." I shake him from his shoulder. "You did not. Do you understand me?"

It was me, I want to shout. I killed her with my arrogance and stubbornness. With my resentment and my thoughtless need to fill my craving for something peaceful.

But I cannot bring myself to say it out loud. Something holds me back from confessing to him.

Instead, I just sigh. "Go home, Cyril. Forget all this."

I wish I could steal the memory out of him somehow. But all I can do is guide him back out the door and into the rain. I shut it on him, before he can ask me anything else.

From the window, I see him stumble away through the rain, back toward the village. Lighting pierces the sky overhead.

Chapter Sixteen

FINALLY THE CLOUDS GIVE and it rains over the village. I put off going into town because of it, but it is still relentless the next day. I know I have to just go and face the downpour.

I have to know if the others remember, and what they are saying.

Besides, the quiet and emptiness of this place, so far removed from everything else, leaves too much room for the necklace to tempt me.

So I brace myself and head out into the torrent. Water pools and flows in streams along the path, soaking my feet through.

When I finally trudge through the mud and reach the village, it is all but empty. The weather has kept most people away.

I go straight to Shara. She will have the goods I must trade for, along with the latest rumors rumbling through the town.

"Nia, my dear!" She watches me approach. "Come, come, under the awning!"

Out of the rain, my skin chills and rises in little bumps.

"Shara," I greet her. "What weather."

"They all begged for the rain. I warned them, do not mess with the gods, do not make demands of them. And now, they have their rain." She waves her hand out into the flooding streets as if she had foretold exactly this. "They do not listen."

I give her a small smile in acknowledgment.

"And my dear, I am so sorry. I heard your mother has passed. Is it true? What happened?"

Curiosity quivers in her eyes buried below the empathy. Good—if she does not know, the rumors must not be flying yet—or else the accounts are so strange and confused they cannot be relied on. I will take either.

"Yes, may she rest in peace," I say.

"May she rest in peace," she echoes, pressing Theia's blessing into her forehead—her goddess—followed by Gloros' over her heart, for my mother's faith.

I copy her gestures before continuing.

"It was a terrible, strange accident. Some villagers were out front with her. To—to help with the fields. But the heat, and then the liquor was passed around...she and the others were joking and tussling, and then Mother just...." I pause, try to look as stunned as I can. "She stumbled back and slammed into the house. Shattered the window completely. She went down, and she didn't get up."

I drop my eyes to the dirt. Let the heavy patter of the rain tell the rest.

Shara gasps.

"Yes," I agree. "Cyril was nearest to her when it happened. He came back to me yesterday. He blames himself. He should not."

There. Anything Cyril says now will not be listened to. The tight anxiety that has constricted me all morning loosens.

"Another terrible tragedy for your family that only the gods could explain." Shara eyes me slyly. "Well. But what is there to say?"

She tuts and shakes her head. Then, she shifts back to her usual businesslike self. I suppose a family tragedy only gains me back a fraction of her esteem.

"But what brings you out to my cart on this gloomy day of misfortune?"

"Meat," I say, dropping my bags of grains on the table.

We conduct our trades.

When I turn to leave, some villagers have collected between Shara's booth and my way home. Most of them were there when it happened.

Only days ago, they lived to adore me. Now, they stand in the furious rain, arms folded and eyes glaring. I hesitate at the edge of Shara's awning. But they are not under the charm's influence anymore. Now they are just men. My neighbors.

I do not know which is scarier, considering the restless way they watch me.

"What happened, Nia?" Ferris calls to me as I pass. He is looking better; the swelling is gone from his face and his color is returning. "What did we do to your mother?"

I turn and approach them, trying to walk slowly to show they cannot intimidate me.

"You did nothing. You were drunk." I start telling them the same story I told Shara. It will be easier later when the rumors begin to spread if the stories are the same.

"You were all tussling around. Then my mother lost her balance and hit her head terribly."

Do I look sad enough to sell it? I look to the ground and try to muster a tear, though I have never been one to cry much, and I do not know if they would see it in the midst of so much rain.

"No," Ferris says. "Liar. We all saw it. It is like a strange warped dream, but we all remember the same. Cyril pushed her. Why would he push her, Nia? Why would you hide it for him? Why is it so hard to remember?"

The others are spreading from behind Ferris, forming a half-circle around me.

"And what about me? What happened to me, Nia? That was at your farm too, whatever it was. Why was I there at all? Why were any of us there?"

"You—to help my mother with the fields."

Ferris scoffs. "I am a metalworker! What do I know of wheat? Do not lie, Nia. You only make it worse for yourself."

"Stop. You are confused." I suddenly wish he did have to follow my commands.

"No, witch." Ferris spits the words at me. "We understand perfectly."

I stiffen. "What does that mean?"

"The gods punished your family once with the Great Illness," Ferris says. "And now they have done it again. One has to wonder—what have you done that your family is cursed in this way?"

"Firstie-lover." Another voice chimes in from farther back. I do not see who.

"I don't know what happened the other night," Ferris hisses, "but we can all see it was more than an accident."

"The gods are against your family," Hector chimes in. "And we're here to remove you from our village."

The others edge in closer, almost surrounding me. My heart is pounding in my ears, drowning out the hard rain.

I turn and try to get away, but a hand grabs a fistful of hair and tugs me back. After that it is a blur of hot bursts of pain as I am tossed and jostled between them. I trip and fall to the ground and they resort to hard kicks from wherever they can make contact.

"Hoi!" a stern voice shouts. *Shara.* "Enough! Or I will call the council."

Through the rain and the feet and the pain, she sounds so far away. But they stop.

"We will finish this later, witch," a final kick to my side.

I moan in response, too sore for anything else. I hear the slosh of steps through mud as they go away, and then one lone pair of feet approaches. A hand softly brushes hair away from my face.

"Thank you."

"Are you all right?" Shara's voice is grudging. She nudges at me with her foot.

"No, no, I am all right." I say it because I want to believe it, and once I say it, it is true enough.

I push myself up to a sitting position. Pain throbs in splotches all over my body. I need help.

"Can you bring Bastus?"

She stares at me a moment, a wash of warmth flickering briefly behind her cold stare. "I thought surely you of all people must know—Bastus has disappeared."

It is a blow more painful than any of the others' attacks. "Disappeared?"

"They say he never came to prayer yesterday, or again today. When they checked his house, his things were gone. Some are saying he must have been called back. Like Calipher."

I do not think so. He has left. Because of me.

But there is no use in saying anything. There is no use in looking for him. He could be anyone by now, whatever he chooses to be. If Bastus does not want to be found, he will not be.

I clench my hands into fists to stop them from shaking, and force myself slowly to my feet. Shara helps me pick up my things.

"Thank you," I say as she hands me the last of it. "Truly. I do not know what would have happened here if not for you."

"You be careful," she chides. "Everything is going wrong, and people are getting scared. This is only the beginning of it. Mark my words."

Chapter
Seventeen

By the time I reach home, I am buckled over from the swelling bruises pulsing over my sides, padding forward as softly and slowly as I can. I am so soaked through that I do not know if I can ever be truly dry again.

How long can the downpour keep up like this? It is going to drown the crops, and there is nothing I can do about it. At least when it was a drought, Mother could drag jug after jug of water to the crops from the dwindling river. Now there is nothing but to wait it out, and see how bad the damage is.

Climbing into bed and wrapping myself in the blankets seems too painful to bear, so instead I slump into a shaking, achy ball on the floor.

What was that? I have never seen so many people so angry, so vicious. Is Shara right? Is it because of the spreading fear?

I sit and watch as the throbbing pain turns into so many welts under my skin, collects in blues and blacks and sickening greens.

Water puddles on the ground around me. I should mop it up. But what does it matter? There is no one left to care where I sit or how messy the house gets. Calipher was taken from me. My mother is dead. Bastus has left.

And it is my own fault, all of it.

My entire body feels heavy and sluggish, a grey exhaustion taking me over. I hurt, and it is not just from the welts growing over my arms and legs and ribs.

It is as if I have been tugged this way and that, high and low, up and down, too many times. It has strung out my soul beyond its capacity, and it has finally given out. The pain comes at me from all sides, not just my body, but also my mind and my soul. It is greater than me. All-consuming.

A raging fire of passion fueled me through it all, and now that it has burned out all that it has left for me is scorched ashes.

All this to satisfy some curiosity? To swallow up the loneliness?

I have been horrid.

And you have more than paid for it.

What will I do now? How will I keep on? The villagers were right. The gods have frowned on me.

Do not turn on yourself, now, too.

Everything has changed. As if the world has turned upside down. Everything is full of fear. There is so much hate in this small village now. It swells around me like walls, too tall to scale. Like we are being held in a cage.

How will I make it all alone in this ruined realm?

You do not have to be alone. Calipher would not want it.

Calipher did not know what he had created. Bastus was right about that, I am sure of it. He never would have meant for all of this to happen. He would never hurt someone on purpose. He would never hurt *me*.

But it does not matter what he meant. Here I am.

This is exactly what Calipher didn't want for me. *If only he knew what he left me to*, I think bitterly.

Gods, how I miss them. Both of them. If I could undo it all and have them back, before things fell apart, before I ever touched Calipher's wing...I would give anything for that.

But you cannot. All you can do is move forward from where you are.

It is true.

So here we are.

So here we are.

For a pause I stare at the floor. Just pull air in and out, accepting the pain as my ribs expand and contract. Accepting the emptiness of the quiet.

You don't have to feel like this.We could make it stop. You never have to feel like this again.

Yes, I could have a bit of peace back, if I'd only put the necklace back on.

But the price. No, no, no. That is over now.

What else could you possibly lose at this point?

I shut my eyes. Everything hurts, in my body and deep into my soul. I am tired and weary and burned. Just the idea of Calipher's aura pulsing through me again is like a sweet aloe.

I only took it off for Bastus anyway, and look what good it has done—none at all.

And now he has abandoned me, and I am so completely broken down from all that has happened that I can hardly stand to move.

A seed of outrage stretches and grows through me.

Calipher would not want this for you. He wanted you happy.

Calipher. Who loved me and wanted me to have everything. Who never told me I was wrong, who never scolded me. And I'm going to hide away his gift for someone who has done just the opposite, and then abandoned me?

No.

I push myself off the dusty ground and pull a chair over to the cupboard, stretch up on top of it to get all the way to where I hid the box. It takes a few tries to push up on my tiptoes and nudge the box out to where I can finally grasp it in my hand. Even just holding the box close to me is enough to start making me feel better. The heaviness in my chest begins to ease and the house doesn't look quite so dark anymore.

When I place the sparkling chain around my neck, the magic slides into me. It is such a great relief I sigh.

It is even more than I remembered. It fills me with peace. It is as if Calipher stands just behind me. My grief and sadness and anger all begin to break away.

I sit and let its magic heal me. By nightfall, the pain is gone and all I can feel is his presence, the peace. All else is nothing.

I will never take it off again.

CHAPTER EIGHTEEN

WITH THE NECKLACE ON, everything becomes easy. For the first time in my life, the restraint breaks away and I feel as if I am gliding.

It is not that I do not hear the names the others call me when I go into the village. Or that I do not see the expressions on their faces as they step back. But the necklace is like a veil around me, and their mutterings are too separate from me to matter. They are only jealous of how their partners adore me. Or the way Calipher favored me over them.

Over time I come to the village less and less—why bother, with so many eager to do it for me?

The realm slowly falls apart. When word reaches us of the First Creatures banding together against the gods, nothing is able to shock us anymore. The villagers are simply too overheated and sun-drained.

Some shrug and get on with their lives. But others, they hold the gods responsible for the tempestuous weather. I cannot blame them—the earth is crumbling apart below our very feet from dehydration. How much more can we bear? How much more will They ask of us?

Some are ready to leave everything to go join the First Creatures in their fight. Rumors float that the First Creature rebels are in a neighboring village and it is like an ember landing on dried straw—a fire engulfs us. The village begins to scatter in the wind, carrying the fire with them. No being, they say, has the right to limit another. Not with Will, not with rules, not with the Texts. And they will fight with the others to stop it. The unrest of the town, a toxic mix of fear and anger, lasts only days as the people pack their things and set off their separate ways. It feels like a tornado has swallowed us up.

The weather too, gets wilder and wilder by turns, storms and droughts, always furious.

But my admirers stay with me.

With the necklace around my neck, I am safely cocooned from it, and it does not matter to me what the weather does. Or the town.

The necklace whispers its secrets to me, and I learn how to keep the admirers under control. How to command them to do my bidding. How to temper their edginess by bringing them to my bed. It keeps the fear and loneliness of the world from swallowing me up.

This was what he wanted. He wanted you to be loved, and look, you are adored by all of them, the necklace whispers. It is true.

All is good. All is easy and painless.

By the time my belly begins to swell, it is impossible to know who the father is. And I do not care. This strange thing growing within me is like a foreign invader, unwelcome and slowly taking me over. Even from behind the veil of the necklace, a thread of fear sneaks into me.

CHAPTER NINETEEN

THE MONTHS PASS IN a blur.

Finally the baby comes, in a furious toil of terror and sweat that goes all through the night. Peri comes to me and helps me through it. Gods bless her, she's stood by the village through it all, even as the other First Creatures have abandoned us, and taken on duties as an ambassador to all the gods, not just Gloros. At first her aura amplifies my fear at what is happening, but she uses her powers to lessen my distress and my pain.

When finally she takes it from me and cleans it, she sighs.

"Oh, Nia, how could you?"

"What?"

Even through the soothing aura of the necklace, labor took too much out of me. I lie on the bed and wait for her to come to me.

But she does not say anything more. She simply places my baby girl in my arms. She is beautiful. She is perfect.

She looks up to me with blank, ice-blue eyes that are all too familiar.

"Oh." It is all I can muster.

"He would never have left, if he knew, I am sure of it," Peri says. "He would come now."

"No!" Panic seizes me. "Peri, swear it to me that you will not tell him. He cannot know."

The last thing I want is for Bastus to come crawling back to me out of some sense of duty, to pin him here to this place he has escaped. The question creeps into my mind despite myself—does Peri know where he is? I cannot bring myself to ask.

Peri stays until finally I talk her into leaving. My admirers can take care of me. These days, there is great need for her out in the world, so many other things for her to tend to in Gloros' name. Besides, she reminds me of days long past, when everything was simpler. It causes a strange fuzzy ache somewhere deep under all my layers.

Before she leaves, she comes and sits at the edge of my bed. "Nia, there is one more thing we must discuss."

I know what is coming. I have been waiting for it.

"I am not giving up the necklace."

She hid it well, but I knew it must be on her mind.

"Nia, it throws off the balance of magic throughout the realm. But forget that, even. Look what it has done to you. Come now. What would your old self think to see you now? And of what's happened to the village?"

"I thought you of all people would understand," I snap. "Are you not a champion of the passions?" I gesture to the admirers outside.

"These are not the true passions of the soul. They are false, and they are feeding on you. They are hurting the entire realm. Just look at all that is happening."

I cross my arms and stare at her petulantly.

She sighs.

"I knew where this would end. But I had to try."

She flutters her wings and floats to the door. "I am disappointed, Nia. Greatly so."

A thick mist of guilt surrounds me as Peri watches me for a moment. Then she is gone, and it is just me and the child. The guilt condenses in thick, swelling drops of fear that cling to everything.

Forget her, the necklace whispers. Who is she to tell us what to do?

I am afraid to answer.

I slowly fall into new rhythms, caring for the girl. I learn how to feed her and swathe her, how to turn tears into giggling coos.

I name her Varya.

And everything continues on. But now when I bring admirers to my bed, I am too aware of the child. Everything has been tinted a new color since she arrived. Her very presence makes the entire world different. And the world I have created here in our home is no place for a child.

Peri's warning clings to me.

So I take the necklace off. Just to see.

It is a relief when the admirers drift off to other things. But then motherhood sets in like a fog.

The girl never stops crying. *I* hardly stop crying.

Her needs are bottomless, and I am not enough to fulfill them on my own. A film builds between me and the rest of the world, between me and the girl. I cannot connect to her no matter how I try, and she is like a stranger, an invader in my home and my heart. Worst of all is the vast emptiness that takes me over. It is as if I am trapped at the bottom of a deep, deep hole, and there is no one to even hear my screams for help. But I am determined to be present for her. Determined to start doing things right.

I keep waiting to snap out of it, for things to settle into a better place. But it never comes. It goes on like this for days. Weeks. Until I can no longer bear how I am failing her.

Why are you putting yourself through this pain? the necklace whispers. You are not meant for it. We both know how this ends. Come back to me.

I don't try to fight it this time. I forfeit to its will. I am too weak on my own—it is better for Varya that I go back to what I was.

The peace from the necklace slips back into place like it was never gone. The war, the girl, all of the pain falls away. The admirers come back. It is just as it was before.

Behind the necklace's protective hum, I am impervious to the realm falling apart around me. Impervious to the child's shrieks. I go through the motions of caring for her, but she cannot reach me through the necklace's veil anymore. I do enough to keep her alive, to keep her quiet. It is not like the emptiness that walled me in before. This is a comforting detachment, as if Calipher's wings were wrapped around me, shielding me from it all. Sometimes the admirers play with her.

It is somewhere in this time that I begin to notice my face. Years have passed, but my face had not changed at all. It still belonged to that young, wide-eyed girl who dreamed of touching Calipher's wing, and barely dared to do it. It does not match the weary woman I have become. Looking at this face is like peering into the past, almost like time traveling, except that I cannot reach out and fix any of it.

It unsettles me. I try not to look at the mirror after that.

The girl grows faster than I can believe. Have I become so detached from the passing of weeks, months, years? When she was small, her eyes were the only thing that give her away as inhuman. But as she grows, so do her abilities.

One morning I catch her floating buttons off the floor. Another day, I hear her giggling wildly in the kitchen. When I reach her, she is snapping her fingers together to create little poofs of whooshing shadow. Then there is the time she wakes up with my face, and she cannot put it back to her own. All day long my too-young face stares back up at me with her blank eyes. It resets to her own chubby, tear-stained face in her sleep that night.

I love my beautiful, strange girl. But it puts me on edge, these emerging powers inside her. And even when she is not playing with her magic, she is often in the way. She asks questions I would rather leave alone.

"Mama, why are those people always coming?" she asks me one day.

Her blank eyes are wide and eager.

"That is not of your concern," I tell her.

"Why?" Her head tilts, her little curls swinging around her face.

"Because it is Mama's business."

"You do business with them?" she asks.

"Of a sort," I reply.

"Why?"

Always the why's. It gets to where my spirit flinches every time the girl opens her mouth, afraid of what she will ask now. The girl can reach me under the necklace's veil in a way nothing else can.

"For the necklace," I tell her. I hold it out for her to see. "Is it not beautiful? Someday, when I die, it will be yours. Then you will see for yourself."

Deep down under the necklace's veil, something inside me recoils at the thought.

When the girl is five, Peri returns, one last time. She tells me she is taking the girl with her. That she will care for her as she did for me as a girl.

Am I the same failure as a mother that my own was?

I should be sad. Or angry. Something. I try to muster the signs of the emotion. I hug the girl close and say I will miss her. But I do not ask Peri not to do it. Behind the haze the necklace has wrapped me in, all I can feel is relief.

After that, time loses the little meaning it had left. Everything bleeds together into a single stream.

I tell the admirers to take the mirror away. I cannot bear to stare at my too-young never-changing face anymore. It is no longer a face I can recognize, unchanged by all that life has done to me. It is like being a stranger in my own body.

The admirers come and go, and I bask in Calipher's aura. The more I bring them to my bed, the stronger it grows.

The war between the realms continues, I suppose. They bring me stories about the horrors it is wreaking across the realm—fields burned down, cities destroyed, battlegrounds that tear Terath open. But it does not touch me. The necklace sings me into a peaceful stupor, keeping me separate from the rest of the world. It is all too distant and removed to matter.

When I finally hear word the war is over and the gods have subdued the rebels, I cry for the first time in ages. The First Creatures have been banned from Terath forever. I let go of one last drop of hope that I did not realize I was clinging to. How will Calipher ever come back to me now? Part of me didn't even realize I still wished for it until then.

Memories of him begin to haunt me. Sometimes I wake up in the middle of the night, and it feels as though he has just whispered in my ear. I am sure he is there, but when I sit up and look for him, the room is empty except for whatever man is at my side that night.

I tilt my head back and close my eyes. One of the admirers I brought in runs his hand over my side and leans forward to graze his lips over my shoulder—his name is Joseph, I think. It makes it easier to think of Calipher when I close my eyes.

Always, I think of Calipher.

His fingers trace down my body and undo my robe. The second admirer presses into my back as he pulls the robe away. I lean back into him, take in his warmth.

Calipher was not warm like this. Calipher was cool and smooth, like marble. I remember this, I know it, and yet I can only barely remember how he felt against my skin.

There are so many of the admirers now. Taking them two at a time sometimes has become easier. I cannot afford to let the rage build among them—I may see the world through a thick haze these days, but I remember what happened to Ferris. I remember my mother. Besides, it pleases the necklace. When I bring the admirers to my bed it swells with joy, filling me with a tingling pleasure.

Suddenly the air grows tense, like thread strained too tight. Then, I catch a glow of light from the corner of my eye.

A new feeling cuts through the necklace's haze to me—no, a very, very old feeling. A deep, quiet peace, like a stream trickling through the woods. It makes the necklace's haze feel stale and false by comparison.

My heart whispers something I do not dare think—no, that is impossible.

"Nia."

Calipher.

I freeze. I am afraid that if I turn to look at him, he will disappear.

But the entire room floods with his aura, and I cannot resist him long.

"Leave," I order the admirers. They pick up their robes and join the others outside.

I wait until the door creaks closed behind them, then slowly sit back and turn to him. He is just as perfect as ever, his smooth glowing skin and his softly curling hair and strong, outstretched arms. His feathers are completely black now. Like midnight.

"Calipher!" I run to him, not bothering to find my robe. "You are here, you are really here."

His arms wrap around me and all I can feel is the intense peace only he can give me. It makes me woozy, and I hear myself babbling.

"They said all the First Creatures were summoned back, and then they lost the war and the gods banished them from the realm. I thought I would never see you again. I thought...I thought...."

The truth is, I have hardly thought anything in so very long. My words drift away from me and all I can do is press against him. The necklace rubs between us, scratching against my chest.

"I'm sorry, I'm sorry, I'm sorry," he murmurs into my hair. "Some of the others were able to resist and break free, and I tried, oh Nia I tried, but it was so hard to break free from Her Will."

I had heard rumors about such things—Firsts who still roamed Terath, lost and alone, too far fallen to be called back. I blocked them out, unable to bear the questions it brought to the surface about Calipher, and why he had not come back to me.

"You are here now."

"Yes...." The steadiness of his arms falter.

"What is it?" I ask. He used to tell me everything, every fear, every question, every thought.

"Nia, the town. They say things...I did not want to believe them. But those people outside. In here." He gestures to the bed.

My throat tightens. "What about it?"

"My parting gift. It has harmed you." He looks down and traces a finger over the brilliant emerald on my chain.

My chest flushes an angry red around it. I step away.

He does not like us.

"Harmed me? Hardly."

The inches of air between our bodies prickles with intensity. Even just this is enough to separate me from his aura. The necklace's potent buzz fills the void.

"But Nia...." He reaches a hand out toward me.

He made us what we are. The necklace vibrates through me in biting sparks.

I pull away from him. "What have you heard? What is wrong with what I have become?"

He watches me thrash like I am a wounded animal in the forest that he cannot help.

He shakes his head. "They say you have lost yourself."

"If I lost myself," I snap, "it happened when you left me here, all alone, with the world falling apart around me. The necklace saved me."

"But Nia..." he glances to the fools near the bed, still fumbling to get their clothes back on. He shakes his head. "I am so sorry."

I narrow my eyes. "Sorry for what?"

Calipher looks away.

"Sorry for what, Calipher?"

I'm yelling now, my voice throwing back off the walls and out the windows into the night. I'm angry, so angry I could explode.

"It is my fault," he replies.

"Do not get self-righteous on me. You have hardly been Theia's good little angel through all this. All I have done since you left is what you said you wanted for me—to wear this necklace, and let others love me since *you* were not there. You were not there, Calipher. *You were not there.*"

I want his cheeks to flush, for his face to crumple into that terrible frown, for him to yell, for him to throw something—anything to show he will fight for me.

All he does is nod, his eyes fixed on the floor.

"You are right. I was not there, and that is what you needed most from me. I have failed you. I have failed you most terribly."

"Please, Calipher, "

I don't know what I'm trying to say, only that I'm suddenly very afraid of losing him all over again. Losing him forever this time. It was one thing to be separated from him, but this look in his eyes. It's an entirely new kind of loss.

"What is it that you want from me?"

"I don't know," he replies. "I really don't."

"I will do anything. Do not leave. Not again."

He looks into my eyes and I beg him, empty my soul out to him. His expression softens.

"Maybe. Maybe it is not too late." He stretches out his hand. "Nia, give me the necklace. We will destroy it. Maybe then, maybe your heart can heal and we can be us again."

"The necklace?" You too, Calipher? My hand grabs the emerald instinctively.

He gave this to me, and now because he does not love how it worked out, he wants to just take it back? Perhaps he should have thought of that before leaving us. Before stealing another god's magic to mess with. Before disappearing for ages, only to judge what we did in his absence, the necklace hisses in my mind. And then I realize—I am saying it all out loud, too. Screaming it, and thrashing out against his impenetrable chest. When I finish, the air swells with hateful silence.

When he finally speaks, his voice is devoid of emotion.

"It is not only about the necklace, Nia. *I know.*"

His eyes widen, as if implying something of great significance.

"You know what?"

"I know about Varya. I know where—who—she came from."

His voice breaks over the name. His face twists in an expression I have never seen on him before. Rage? Heartbreak?

"This is different from the others, Nia. The others were all because of the necklace, because of the heartbreak I left you with. I know that. But Bastus, Nia? The necklace would not have worked on him."

It is as if all the weight of emotion I have hidden from all these years grows too heavy all at once. The support gives out, and it all comes crashing down on my head.

"Gods," I exclaim. "What do you want from me?"

"Tell me it is not true," he begs. His eyes are frantic.

"Calipher, you do not understand. It wasn't like that."

I try to find the words to make him understand, to make this all okay, but I cannot find a single one to hold onto.

Meanwhile, his expression is draining, as if his emotions are leaking out of him.

"Calipher, you have got to understand, please."

But it is already over.

All the terrible things we have said, and now this too. I can see it in his face. This is broken far beyond repair. He did not come to reunite. He came to see if it was all true.

The rage explodes inside me all over again. I am angry at him for coming here. Angry that he broke Theia's rules all those years ago. Angry at him for loving me, and angry at him for leaving me. Angry that it took him so long to come back to me, and angry that he is here at all.

Angry at myself, and all my weakness, every step of the way.

I am so angry I could explode. The emerald burns hot and bright against my chest.

His face is solemn. All the heartbreak and anger are gone from it, tucked away with his other emotions in some safe place I cannot reach.

"I am sorry, Nia. You are right. I have ruined it all," he says.

He speaks slowly and gently, as if to a child, who could not possibly know enough to truly understand.

"It is too late for us. But it is not too late for you. Please, take the necklace off."

"We will not!" Before I can respond, the necklace speaks through me. "You cannot separate us! We are one now."

My voice is a hysterical hiss. I am like a puppet as it fights for its claim on me.

But I agree with the words. I cannot go back to what I was before it. I remember what it felt like, that deep endless hole inside me, a pain I could not crawl out from under. I will not give it up again, not ever.

Calipher stretches out his hand and begins to murmur an elaborate chant. A current vibrates through me, and the necklace seizes onto my soul, opposing forces at war within me. A gasp escapes me.

I glare back into his glazed-over eyes.

"No!" I cry.

"No!" the necklace bellows.

"NO!" My will and the necklace's sync, like a cart's wheel aligning into a worn track through the dirt. As the word tears through me and out of me, a stream of sparks flies from my outstretched hand and sends Calipher crashing backward into the wall.

The power is coursing through every particle of my body now, waiting, eager to be used. I wait, my chest heaving, for Calipher to try again. But his wings just droop as his eyes run over me one last time.

"Oh, my Nia." He shakes his head, his eyes brimming deep disappointment—or is it fear? "I am so sorry."

He reaches out and I flinch, afraid he will go for the necklace again, but he simply strokes my cheek. A rush of pure peace washes over me, and for just a moment, it drowns out the strange power that flooded me. I close my eyes as I lean into his hand, into the stillness. The aura shrinks away, and when I open my eyes, he is gone.

Chapter Twenty

IT IS LIKE SOMETHING in me has been waiting for Calipher to return.

Now that he has come and gone, a great relief breaks over me and a tightness in my stomach dissolves.

It is true freedom. Finally I can give myself over to the necklace completely. I do not have to keep trying to hold onto what I used to be anymore.

The town wants to call me a witch? Then perhaps I will be one. Perhaps I already am one. But witches are feared for a reason. They wield great power. And so do I.

I have grown used to the isolation, just me and my admirers. It cannot hurt me anymore.

The years pile up, decades upon decades. More years than I should have in my natural life. The admirers start to all look the same, and the eternally unchanging face in the mirror haunts me. The necklace's power surges through me, multiplies within me, until my body is weary from it.

I barely leave the bed. Even eating seems pointless.

One day, I pray to Gloros, and my prayer is answered—Peri comes to me soon after.

"Nia," she greets me as I open the door. "Is all well?"

A line presses between her brows, like she knows the answer. She leans away from me, her arms wrapped around herself.

I step aside to let her in. "Thank you for coming."

"You asked for me?" she says.

"I did."

She stands quietly and waits for me to tell her more.

"I am weary, Peri. I am ready for it to be over. But I do not believe I have the strength in me."

Her frown deepens and she tilts her head. But she remains silent, waiting for me to explain.

"Whatever happens, when I give it to you, do not give it back. I need it all to be over, and this is the only way."

She straightens up and shifts her stance, understanding. Her eyes drift to the emerald. "I promise."

Even before I start to reach for it, the necklace begins to claw and tear at my soul.

No, it cries out. We have come too far, we have become too strong.

I wrap my hands around the chain.

You cannot. You WILL not. The voice burns through me, a fire bursting beyond its tinder.

I have to, I plead. It is long past time for my soul to leave this realm, and this is the only way.

No, it hisses back. The chain grows hot-hot-hotter until it singes my skin.

I tug it over my head before I can turn weak and hold it out for Peri to take.

It does not seem to burn her. She cups it between her hands and holds it close.

But a storm still rages inside me. I am burning hot. I am ice cold. I am empty.

The years race to catch up with me. My bones weaken and my muscles shrivel, my joints turn creaky and stiff. My skin dulls, then begins to loosen and crinkle.

"Nia." Peri steps closer and reaches to me, as if she can help in some way.

But I am far past helping. I know that now.

I can end the pain, the necklace rages. Take me back. It is not too late.

I hunger for it. I know from last time that the longer it is off, the greater the pain will get. This is only the beginning.

But, if I am right, it will not last long.

"Go!"

Peri's aura is at work in me, magnifying every terrible emotion wrangling through me. It is too much to bear. The temptation of the necklace too great.

"Go!" The second time it comes out as a terrible shriek, barely still a word at all.

She hesitates, staring as my body writhes and withers.

Then she goes.

As she moves away from me and out the door, the necklace tries to cling to my soul, scraping at the walls of my mind and tugging at my heart.

A last wave of regret rises. I want it back. This emptiness is excruciating. I need to make the pain end. But I am powerless to do so now, thank the gods. All I can do is wait it out.

Eventually dark settles in, I know it is almost over.

It rains that night. Not the furious downpours we are used to these days. A soft patter, almost a mist. I hobble outside on my weakened, old legs and sit on the perch just outside to take it in. It is cool and soothing on my wrinkled skin, like so many tiny kisses.

I lay back and am transported back to that first time in the forest with Calipher, the gentle way the waterfall misted our bare skin as we lay out next to it. My heart's manic beating slows.

The world and all its burdens fade away to nothing, and finally, and finally my restless mind finds peace.

THE END

Keep reading now with MUD, the first book in the Third Realm War series
READ NOW

Keep reading

The Chronicles of the Third Realm War continue

Keep reading now with the first novel in the trilogy, *Mud*

Torn apart by war and abandoned by the gods, only one hope remains to save humanity. But the savior isn't human at all.

Trapped by his Maker's command to protect a mysterious box, Adem is forced to kill anyone who tries to steal it. When a young boy chances upon Adem's temple, he resists temptation, intriguing the golem. As the boy and his sister convince Adem to leave the refuge of his temple, the group lands in a web of trouble.

Now Adem will do whatever necessary to keep his new young charges safe, even if it means risking all to get rid of the box. Their saving grace comes in the form of an angel who offers to set Adem free of the box's magic by granting his greatest desire—making him human.

But first, Adem must bring back the angel's long-dead human love from the Underworld. In doing so, he will risk breaking the barrier between the realms, a cataclysm that could launch the Third Realm War. To set things right, he may be forced to give up the only thing he's ever truly wanted.a chance a

Read now on Kindle Unlimited!

All formats at EJWenstrom.com

Keep reading

Rona didn't ask to be brought back from the dead. Now that she's back, she's angry enough to raise hell.

It's a good thing, too, because hell is coming. When the creature Adem dragged Rona back through the Underworld to Terath, the barriers between the realms shattered, and now demigods are breaking free. Demigods determined to take down the gods and replace them.

Terath is still ravaged from the previous wars between the gods and the demigods, and may not survive another. Already, a powerful sorcereress is working to organize the demigod rebels and harness their rage. But Rona refuses to watch her world be destroyed a second time.

Which means Rona must come to terms with the life she's been dragged back to, and quick. She has no time for the horrific visions of the demigod she once loved, or the way he slowly went made as their love broke his connection to his goddess.

Can she suppress the reckoning of her past long enough to save the entire realm's future?

Read now on Kindle Unlimited!

All formats at EJWenstrom.com

Keep reading

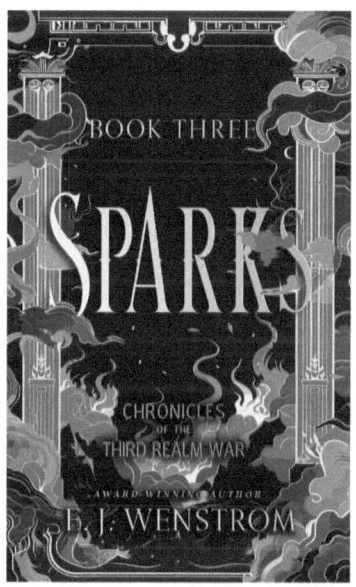

Being Chosen by the Gods doesn't mean much when they have abandoned you.

With a special connection to the gods, Jordan was raised to be the savior of his people. Now that the foretold final war of the realms has arrived, everyone is looking to him—leader of Haven, prophet with a direct connection to the gods' will—for answers.

Demigods are breaking free of the Underworld and picking sides, joining either Jordan's army ordained by the gods, or the rebel forces determined to overthrow them. And now, a new threat rises – a sorcerer more powerful than Jordan thought possible, with a legion of enchanted soldiers at his bidding, who seeks to destroy Haven before the war even begins.

But Jordan is unravelling. How can he tell his people that the gods have fallen silent, just when he needs them most?

And now Adem—Jordan's oldest friend and trusted advisor—has abandoned Haven, believing his curse puts the entire settlement at risk. Jordan can't lead his army to victory alone, so he sets off to bring Adem back. Even if he must break into the gods' own realm to do it.

Read now on Kindle Unlimited!

All formats at EJWenstrom.com

Also by
More from E. J. Wenstrom

Tonight, seventeen-year-old Evalee is scheduled to die.

She's planned her celebration for weeks, and other than leaving her sister Gracelyn behind, Evalee is ready. She shouldn't be nervous; the Directorate says this is how it should be, and it is never wrong. So she wears her best dress and dances the night away with all of her appointed friends and family. Then she goes to sleep for the last time...

Except, the next morning, Evalee wakes up.

Gracelyn is a model Directorate citizen with a prodigious future ahead. If she could only stop thinking about the shuffling from Evalee's room on her departure morning. Even wondering if something went wrong is treason—the Directorate doesn't make mistakes. If she pulls at the thread, the entire privileged life the Directorate set for her will unravel into chaos. Or worse.

Before the Directorate can correct its mistake and get rid of Evelee for good, she is swept away by rebels to a world she grew up believing couldn't exist—one filled with unpredictability and messy choices. As the Directorate's lies are stripped away, Evalee becomes determined to break Gracelyn free from its grasp—before Gracelyn's search for the truth draws the Directorate's attention and makes her more valuable to them dead than alive.

A young adult dystopian adventure perfect for fans of Uglies, Divergent, and The Hunger Games.

"Departures ... delights and disturbs and allows us to see our own world with brand new eyes."
— Lance Rubin, New York Times Bestselling Author

"An absorbing, taut coming-of-age tale that grapples intelligently with mortality and liberty."
—Kirkus Reviews

"Wenstrom's masterful storytelling is on full display with rising stakes, tense twists, and emotional resonance."
—Megan Lynch, Award-Winning Author

Sneak Peek: Mud, Chronicles of the Third Realm War

Chapter 1

A stair creaks.

With the rain pounding down on the temple's rattling roof, the human may not have even heard the sound. But I do. It is too close, just outside the door of my tower. I look up from the Texts and listen.

There it is again.

A cold darkness tosses in my stomach. I know I'm about to kill again.

Over the centuries, I've at least learned how to make it quick. My hand has already dug the box from the breast pocket of my cloak. I stride across my small room, my bare feet collecting dust. My back to the door, I lean on the mantle to lure the Hunter in. Then, I stare at the blank dusty wall and wait. The rustle of his cloak breaks the quiet with each step.

I hold the box high in my hand for him to see, as if I am inspecting it. So small, so delicate. It nestles easily against my palm, comfortable and sure. It knows I must serve it.

Padded steps lift from the wood and onto the worn rug. Dread, heavy and thick like a storm cloud, wells up inside me. Have they learned nothing from their many losses? So many I cannot count them anymore.

I lay the box on the mantle for him to reach. I will not destroy the human of my own will. He must bring it on himself. I step away from it, leave it there for the Hunter to set his fate.

A rustle of rushed steps, a grunt, and a blade slices through my back, cool and slick. They keep trying to hurt me as if I were human, as if I felt the pain like they do. I reach around and remove the blade from my back. The skin knits itself back together.

I turn to him. Rain beats at the window. Wild dilated eyes peer up at me from under a deep red hood. Young. The cloak slips at his neck, too large for his growing body. It is the same deep red cloak all the others wore. Rich velvet, with the same gold braided trim. My own cloak, worn and ripped, seems even worse next to it.

The boy is trembling inside it. Waiting.

Has he even experienced a true fight before? Why did they send someone so young?

"It's not too late. Leave." My voice is rough with disuse.

I shift the knife in my hand, holding it away to show him I don't mean him any harm, not if I can help it.

Like their cloaks, the Hunters' blades are fine, an elaborate pattern carved into its handle. I run my fingers over its familiar ridges and wait.

He gapes up at me, my monstrosity. I fight the urge to drop my gaze to the ground and instead keep my eyes locked on his. I try to will him to turn away, to go back to wherever he came from.

But I already know he won't. They never do.

Instead, he gives himself a quick shake and recovers his warrior's front. "The Sworn will not rest until it is destroyed. Give me the box."

Courage glows in his eyes. Strong. Fresh. What a waste of a life.

The Sworn? What is the Sworn?

"I cannot."

If only I could. It would save both of us.

He reaches for the box on the mantle.

"Don't—"

His fingers wrap around it.

The force of the box's curse takes over and my arms reach for him. I wince as my hand slips the Hunter's own blade through his soft middle.

He gasps, clasps his hands to his open belly, trying to hold it in. Then he slumps to the floor, spilling his life across the wooden panels. He opens his mouth to gasp, but it comes out as more of a gurgle, blood rising in his throat.

Not much time left. I try to push down the throbbing anger, the monster in me that hungers for the fight. I kneel beside him, gripping his head urgently so he is looking at me.

I hold the box to his face. "What is in it? Why do you come for it? Who are the Sworn?"

A red line dribbles down his chin. He looks up at me, trembling, shakes his head side to side.

"You don't know?"

His words come out in a hoarse whisper. He is shaking all over now in a struggle for his life. He opens his mouth again, tries to push out more. But the dark puddle grows fast below him, and it is over before it begins. Again, I am alone in the heavy dark of the temple tower.

The Hunter's eyes are cold and dead and open wide.

Watching, judging, condemning.

And they should. They have seen what I am.

I used to tell myself I would get used to it. I got used to snapping bones, last cries, pools of blood. But the eyes. The eyes freeze in an echo of their final panic and pain. When they realize these are their last breaths. Paled. Filmed. Hollow.

The Hunter's eyes stare up at me and I can't bear it.

I step out onto the balcony to escape them. Try to clear my head. Rain squeezes out of the sky like teardrops over the cobblestone streets in the marketplace below, over the thin rotted roofs of the laborers' quarters beyond it, over the wall that traps them within the city's borders. Even over the city center, where Epoh's elite rest, safe and dry. It pounds down on me, drop, by drop, by drop.

So close, yet again.

I set the box next to me on the railing, run a finger the curves of the delicate patterns painted over it. Such beauty. But it's what's inside that the Hunters come for, die for. That much I know. If only it would open. If only I knew what my body betrayed me for, why my hands are covered in blood yet again.

They will send another. They always do. I will be waiting. It goes without end, back further than I can remember. Years trudge by, bodies pile up, the weight grows heavier.

I cling to my new clue. *The Sworn.* The phrase is meaningless to me, but it is more than I had before. Next time, maybe I can learn even more.

Already the dark sky is lightening toward a troubled gray. Another weary day is here in the city of Epoh.

Which means I'll be stuck with the Hunter's cold stare all day. There's no time to move the body now. Soon Epoh's Silencers will be out, the city's guards who keep the order with fear and clubs. Ever since they burned down the Holy District and all the Texts so many years ago, anything related to the Three Gods makes them jump. Any sign of movement from a temple like this would trigger a full search of the grounds. Then where would I go? There's nothing else left beyond Epoh's walls. Nowhere else to go.

It wasn't always like this. The realm was happy once. There were tons of other cities in the realm, and they were thriving. But something shifted in the Second Realm War.

Some say the Three saw the destruction and anger and hate that spread throughout the realm of Terath in the Second Realm War and abandoned it. Others say the Three themselves were on the battlefield, and They came with Their soldiers to beat at Epoh's wall, begging to be let in and shown a little of kindness—care for wounds, a drink of water—but the people would not let them in for fear of the rebels. Others say the Gods simply saw how few men dared fight for Them and turned away.

Whatever it was, the Gods are gone, and the people won't dare invoke Them for anything, afraid of Their wrath. The realm is in ruins. Only the Gods know what lies beyond Epoh's high walls. If They care enough to look.

That's why I hide here, in the temple. I keep to where the humans don't dare wander. The Gods don't worry me. They forgot this realm long ago.

I force myself back inside and step toward the body. I drag my fingers over the grayed lids to close them. I pull his cloak from under him to mop up the congealing blood from the floor. With his eyes off of me, my entire body finally begins to relax again.

It must be such great relief, knowing you can end. I envy them that, the humans. But not like this. Not before your time. Not alone, with no chance.

When I'm done with the floor, I lay the cloak over the body. His legs jut out at the end. The eyes still haunt me through the cloth. But there's no time to do anything more.

I pick up the Texts from the mantle and move quickly past the body to the window, trying to push the Hunter out of my thoughts. Below my feet the ornate rug, once rich and brilliant, is worn so deep I can feel the wood's grain under my toes. Decades of standing in the same place day after day after day. Here, I am in the shadows. A human peering in from the streets would not see me. But I can see out.

I watch them. Completely alone, silent, still, there is nothing else to do.

My temple tower rears up against what's left of the holy district, tall and tired, leering over the market. I watch each day play out on its wide streets and small carts. Behind it, the expired grandeur of the aged towers rises, a rotted reminder of a lost past.

There was a time when Epoh was Terath's shining jewel. Its streets bustled with life at all hours. But the Second Realm War changed everything. The First Creatures tore through the realm like it was paper, their battles destroying men's cities, homes, the land itself. And the humans, they took part. Some stood up and fought for their Gods. But others turned away from them in anger. Others' loyalty was easily bought with magic, jewels, or promises of safety after it all ended. Still others ran, cowered, and just waited for it to end.

I'd never, in all my years, seen such destruction.

This is when Zevach arrived at Epoh, with his flock trailing behind him, desperate to believe his promises of protection and hope. Then Zevach told his followers if they wanted the city, they must take it for themselves. Desperate and scared, they fought their way in and destroyed most of its people.

They should have known then what he would become, that this was the city's fate. I should have.

The sky turns from pitch black to a troubled gray. The rays of light touch over the battered city. Silencers' boots tap against the pavement. Another weary day in Epoh is here.

Chapter Two

Every day is the same. There is no rest.

The Silencers are the first to take the streets. Zevach's trained men, guards he collected to protect the people he brought here in the Second Realm War. In the beginning, they watched the city's borders and made sure nothing got in. But when the war was over, they turned their eyes and their weapons inward. Zevach told the people the Silencers were here to keep the peace. But all they sow is fear.

Each morning the Silencers circulate through the roads and alleys, clinking in their armor, their heavy black boots tap-tap-tapping through the fog before curfew lifts. Steam pours from their mouths like dragons in the damp morning freeze.

As the sun pulls itself up, the rain tapers down to nothing. Shopkeepers drag their wooden carts to their usual places along the sides of the street and arrange their displays, pulling their cloaks around them tight.

Soon the laborers come. The ones who grow the food, sew the clothing, create the luxury items for the city's elite. They flood the streets in a rush to get the day's meals before shift. Tired, beaten. Their trampled voices throw off tower walls and bounce up to me amid the morning quiet.

Inside the teeming mass, a young boy with bright red hair stands very still. He stares up at my tower. He can't possibly see me, not from all the way down there. But still his stare prickles behind my ears like pins. Ever since he and a few others slipped into my temple through a shattered window, he does this.

It happens, sometimes. Just restless laborers' children curious about the things no one talks about, mostly. Sometimes the helpless get desperate and come here hoping the Gods will listen. I keep to my tower, and soon they are gone again.

Except this time. This time they had climbed the tower stairs. They had explored every room. Anxiety had spread over my shoulders and down my back as their hushed voices crept closer and closer up the tower, pausing at each room on the way. I had buried the box in my pocket and hovered in the room's darkest shadows.

When finally they reached the top and swung open my door, I had tried to be as small as I could, tried to let the shadows swallow me. But there had been no hiding. As soon as they saw me, the other boys had gasped and fled. But the red-haired boy, he had stayed. He had stepped closer. He had reached his hand toward me, fingers stretched and palm out as if feeling for something. He had frowned as he looked me over.

"What are you?" he had asked.

The other boys seem to have forgotten. They never look to the temple. They don't dare go near it, or anywhere on the Holy District's border. It is only this one, this boy with the red hair. He looks up at my window and his face reminds me how quickly I could lose it all.

What are you?

The question grates and scratches along the walls of my mind. All he has to do is tell someone I am here, and I will forced out the temple, out of Epoh, into the wastelands beyond the wall.

But now the other boys call to him and pull him back to the street. They greet him with grins and friendly slaps to his shoulder. Before they run off, the boy runs to a woman and pulls on her skirt. She always comes to market with him. She leans down and says something to him, her fiery braid swinging off her shoulder. In a different world, one where life had not wrung so much out of her, she would have been beautiful. She turns away and begins her morning shopping at a nearby cart.

The boy turns and races toward the middle of the street with the others. They split up, their eyes glued to the streets. The boy pushes against the flow of traffic, hardly noticing as the others shove and knock him as they pass. It takes only a few minutes, and with a shout to the others, he dives under the crowd. He emerges victorious, waving a flat smooth stone over his head.

They cheer. The stone is dropped back to the ground and the boys kick it back and forth, weaving through the morning shoppers. While the rest of Epoh drag themselves awake and brace for another day of work and abuse, the boys play. Some of the shoppers frown, even snap at the boys as they rush past. Others crack a rare, weak smile. The boys tease, laugh, and run free through the streets.

Free. In Epoh.

The tension in my shoulders loosens as their laughter floats up. I drink it in while I can. It can't last long. The woman will return and call him back any moment.

The more they play the more they forget themselves. The boys get bolder, run faster, call louder, leave Epoh far behind. Their calls throw off the cement, brick, glass, and race toward the sun's open arms. Escape into the sky.

No one escapes.

A knot tightens between my shoulders. They will pay for this if a Silencer catches on.

One already has. Tall, with a furrowed brow and jutted jaw. His club is already clenched tight in his hand. Hungry for action. He wafts in the tail of their shouts, trailing behind. Waiting for his moment.

They have done nothing wrong.

It will not matter.

But any moment the woman will step out from the carts, give a shout, and the boy will be back by her side. They will walk away together. The stone will lay still in the streets again, trampled by passers-by. The play will dissolve.

She should be back any moment.

Where is she?

The streets are swarmed, but I cannot see her in them.

There it is—a glimpse of flashing red. Behind the crowd, in line at a shop-keeper's cart. I strain to peer through the stream of passing workers, my fore-head pressing into the glass. She waits, her arms juggling too many things. At the front of the line, a man waves wildly at the store clerk, his face flushed a deep red.

Meanwhile, the boys are still playing. Every call, every laugh winds the tension in me tighter and tighter now, trapping me in a coil, squeezing too tight. The Silencer trails them, wafting in the wake of their cheers. Still the woman could appear and with one call shatter the moment into pieces, pieces too small for the

Silencer to pick up. But she is still waiting in the line. The game continues, and the Silencer is closing in.

A hard kick sends the stone flying. It spins overhead, floating, soaring, and bounces off the Silencer's head.

The moment seeps in, steals the grins from the boys' faces, and sinks into the crowd around them. It spreads across the Silencer's face and drips like poison from the thin smile crossing his lips. The Silencer picks up the stone. He rolls it over in his hand, holds it out to the nearest boy to come take.

And suddenly the boy looks so, so small. Small except his eyes, which are huge, bulging with fear. A fear that traps him to the spot where he stands. The Silencer's sharp jaw tightens and grinds behind his grin as he waits.

The boy slowly steps toward the Silencer, his face tense and blank. Nearby shoppers step away, make room, as if the moment will combust. When the boy is near enough, he reaches out cautiously for the stone. He almost gets it.

At the last moment, the Silencer's smile disappears and he snatches the stone away and grabs the boy's arm.

Through a clenched jaw, he growls with anger: "I'll teach you to get in the way of a Silencer of Epoh."

The crowd watches in horror. The Silencer lifts his club above his head and whips it down, striking the boy across the face. No one moves. No one speaks. No one stops it. It happens all the time like this.

He lifts it again, his expression loaded with hate.

Suddenly something jostles through the crowd from one side, and before the Silencer can strike again the fiery-haired boy has pushed in front of his friend, is taking his blow.

A flood of words spill from him onto the Silencer. "Stop it! Leave him alone—"

The Silencer snarls, forgets the other child, and grabs the redhead by his shirt. He spits out words sharp as blades inches from the boy's face.

"Stop? Are you telling *me* what to do?" The Silencer shakes the boy. "How dare you use such a tone with a guard chosen by Zevach. Maybe you need a lesson more than your friend."

Then he strikes. Again. Again. Again. Each time staining the stick redder as the blood pools and drips from the child's face. The boy cries out.

The crowd jostles again and the woman is now at its center behind the Silencer. Too late. When she sees, she screams and runs to the boy, pulls him back from the Silencer's wrath.

"How dare you." Her words spit out in sharp tones of jagged glass. "He's just a boy! Don't you ever touch my brother again."

In the moment she has while the guard is stunned, she frantically checks the boy's face, brushes back the fire-red hair, runs her hands over his head. She crumples to her knees and wraps her arms around the boy, presses her face against his shoulder. And then she forgets herself in her relief, she must forget herself, or she would know better than to do what she does next.

"Thank the Gods," she says.

The words are quiet. Most of the humans don't hear it. Only a few of those closest look up. But as soon as the words escape her lips, as soon as the first accusing eyes flit to her, her cheeks burn red. The whispers travel like lightning and soon the whole square is buzzing, followed by deadly silence and stares. Her flush spreads, covering her face and down her neck. Burning hot, angry, and defenseless.

No one, no one, no one invokes the Gods. Not in Epoh. It is a death wish.

I clutch the Texts in my fist tight and battered, afraid of what will happen next, unable to look away. The woman's words still float heavy in the air. An awful blackness builds in my chest, coursing through me and into my head, my fingers, my toes, filling me, emptying me, consuming me. Helpless.

The Silencer's flat eyes ring with sadistic joy.

Still clasping the child, the woman whips around and pulls him behind her into the crowd. I follow the trail of jostling bodies as long as I can. It could be the last time I see her.

The Silencer doesn't bother to follow. He stands watching as they run. He knows there's no rush. Even if she escapes now, they will find her later. There's only so much space to search inside Epoh's walls. She will be a warning to the others to keep their minds on their own realm. Her best hope is that they will be carried away early on, and she will die quickly.

They'll take the boy too. Throw him in training to be a Silencer as they've done with so many others. He will forget his home, his family, whatever the woman has been teaching him about the Gods. He will come back blank-faced and cold.

But for now the show is over, and the crowd begins to move again, tending to their business. The rest of the day passes quietly. I watch without seeing as the laborers leave, the elite make their leisurely strolls through the carts in bright fresh tunics and cloaks. The Silencers step down, becoming less harsh when the elite shop.

Finally, the market dies down, the shopkeepers pack up their days work, the sun sets, and the Silencers forfeit the streets to the dark. Night settles in as it always does, over empty streets that have already forgotten what happened this afternoon. But my hands are still clenched in anxious fists, nails digging into my palms. Epoh hasn't forgotten what happened. The Silencer hasn't forgotten. Fear rattles in my chest when I think of what's in store for the fiery-haired boy and his sister.

Chapter Three

At the other end of the room, the cold stare of the Hunter's corpse watches me through his cloak. I want it out, buried deep, deep, deep, so deep even I could never find it again.

Outside, the day is done, but I let another hour pass before daring to move. I wait for signs that Epoh's underworld is stirring, to be sure none who would care are here to see me haunting the temple's empty halls. The box is still gripped tight in my hand, so tight its pointed corners pierce into my skin. So tight the tension pulls on my knuckles. So tight it should break.

If only it would break.

Once the shadows start lurking in through the alleys, I know I'm safe.

Even through the blanket, those cold, knowing eyes send quivers down my back. I brace myself and step toward it, and quickly sling it over my shoulder, sheet, and all.

It is surprisingly light for such a great burden.

I open the door from my tower and make my way down the cold stone steps to the temple's sanctuary. The air trapped in its dark pockets is thick with dust and memory. So many bodies I've already carried down these winding stairs.

The sanctuary is an abrupt burst of light at the end of the stairs. Full moon tonight. It pushes through the temple's stained-glass windows, spills fractures of blue, purple, red, and green. The pews awaken beneath its light and the pulpit is restored to its former glory. I quicken my stride as I walk across the back of the room to the wooden door at the other end.

The door creaks as I push it open. The rich smell of sod beckons and repels me. I force through the door's small frame and the dark swallows me back into its comfortable emptiness. The old stairs groan under my weight. I tread over the compact earth of the cellar's floor, past the rows of raised mounds in the ground, each marking a life gone. A life I took.

I feel each one below my feet. I remember. Down here they will always be freshly murdered, their blood still warm and sticky on my hands.

This easy deposit is one of the reasons I've stayed here so long. The Hunters would have found me anywhere. They have not always been so easy to hide.

I reach the row's end and release the body to the ground. My fingers sink easily into the dirt. Cool and rich. I crumble handful after handful and push it away, lulled into an easy rhythm.

The body drops into the hole with a soft thud. I fold the dirt back over him, smooth it out.

He didn't deserve this. To be hidden away, forgotten.

On top of the mound, I push in a small dot with my thumb to mark where he lies. The symbol of the temple's Goddess Theia—a seed. It is the least I can do; leave him with some kind of blessing. Maybe it makes no difference, if the Three have really abandoned Terath. But maybe not.

Going back, I move quicker. My eyes have adjusted to the dark and I don't have to rely on memory.

Past the long line of the dead.

Up the whining stairs.

Through the door—and I freeze.

Something is wrong. Through the half-opened door, a flickering light bounces off the atrium wall. Not the diluted colors of the temple's colored panes. Pure, clear, white. Flickering...like a candle.

There's humans in here.

Humans, here in my temple. To be wandering the night in Epoh, they must be reckless. To be here, in this place of the Gods, they must be completely desperate.

I don't dare move. The stairs are too loud for retreat—it's a miracle they did not already hear me. I cautiously pull the door back in best I can, and watch their flickering shadows on the wall, distorted and strange, through the crack.

Their whispers magnify off the walls. A man and a woman. Her voice quivers, matches the faded sanctity of this place. His is gruff and hurried as he pushes himself in through the broken sanctuary window.

"We shouldn't be here," he growls. "We should go."

"By the Gods, you will stay."

"I can do this ritual just as well in my tent—"

"No." Her voice sparks like flint. "You will do it here. In Theia's house. Where the conduit to Them is strongest."

The voice is familiar. It hovers in my ear, waiting to be known.

The man's shadow moves away from her another step. She closes the gap. When she speaks, again it is so soft it is almost nothing. "Please. In Theia's name, I beg you. My brother—"

"Yes, you told me already. I know." The man's shadow shifts and fidgets. He sighs. "We need to get started. We cannot be here long."

Her shadow nods eagerly.

They move to the front of the sanctuary, their shadows stretching across the back wall. He grows as the stairs to the pulpit creak under him. She kneels to the ground.

They pause: a true silence.

Then the man stretches out his arms, tilts back his head, and becomes a great stretching shadow-tree against the back wall.

"Most holy Mother, Theia the Creator—" The prayer transform his voice, strengthens, deepens it. "Have mercy on your beloved child, who lives in your Order..."

A draft pushes past me, forces the door wide enough to walk through with a loud whine. Anxiety rises in goosebumps over my skin. They heard it, they had to have heard it, and now they will come to see what caused it. They will find me, and all will be lost.

But the man's voice continues to echo through the building without pause: "...we beg you, protect this child from the forces working against your Order..."

I exhale my panic and let it break away into the air.

The woman speaks now, a rhythmic response in the prayer, her voice—that voice I somehow know—rustling down the aisle and tickling my ears, stirring up a restless ache inside me, an ache that unsettles and surprises me.

The door is already open. They are at the other end of the large sanctuary. Her voice tugs at me, and curiosity wins out.

I place my hand on the floor to lean out into the atrium. My arm quivers with caution. Their ritual could end any moment. If I'm going to do it, I need to do it fast.

I push myself forward onto my arm.

I catch just a glimpse before I pull back again. But a glimpse is all I need.

A thick braid twists down the woman's back, a fire-red rope. It's the woman from the market, the one who always comes with the boy. The one who whispered her own death sentence today. My stomach flutters with excitement, confusion, curiosity. Who is this woman, so willing to do these reckless things no one else in Epoh would dare?

I pull back behind the door and lean against the wall. I hope they are done before sunrise so I am not stuck in the cellar with the dead all day. But for now I can only wait. I settle into my spot, close my eyes, and drift into the rhythm of their chanting prayer. It's soothing, somehow. Not just the voices, but also the presence of someone familiar. If only she didn't have to leave. But she does, for both of our sakes.

No wonder she is desperate. Breaking into the temple in the dead of night is nothing to what she already did in the glaring midday. I wonder where the boy is now, how badly the Silencer hurt him. And what horror lies ahead for the woman when they find her. Because there is nowhere they could hide that the Silencers won't soon find.

Something twitches near my arm and pulls me out of my thoughts. As if the air itself pinched. It grows larger, tightening, pulling, and snapping into a tense current. I open my eyes and stand alert, looking for the cause around me in the cellar's darkness.

And then, a blinding light comes from the cellar and washes out everything else.

Chapter Four

I am frozen, caught, blind in the glaring light. Adrenaline charges through me, pulsing in my wrists and pounding my ears.

The light wanes to a low glow, beckoning across the dark cellar, and takes shape.

A figure like a man, but larger. Too perfect, a chiseled marble statue under an airy white robe. Silvery blonde locks curl around a brooding forehead. Skin glows pale and soft as the moon. But a darkness hovers around him—two inky black wings burst from his back.

His eyes glow hot as embers, burn through me with a steady gaze. My fingers wrap around my blade in its hilt, but he reaches out an arm toward me: *All is well.* My body's chaos quiets.

"I am Kythiel, angel of Theia." His voice is pearly smooth.

Theia. The Goddess they used to pray to here.

I blink. An angel, one of the First Creatures. Right here in front of me. They were rare enough before the war, but since then most have understood them to have been locked them out of the realm.

His eyes bore through me, hot with intensity.

"They're upstairs," I say. It comes out weak.

The perfect face clouds into confusion. "What?"

"Theia's followers. They're upstairs." I whisper the words, afraid they will hear us.

"*Theia's* followers?" he scoffs. "I am here for myself. I am not Her mindless slave like some of the others. Those worshippers' prayers merely opened the way for me. I came here for you, chthonus."

It doesn't make sense, and my mind won't wrap around it.

"But—"

"Stop it. Be still."

He circles me slowly, those burning eyes passing over my every inch.

"And you needn't whisper, by the way," he chuckles. "I've taken care of it. Simple charm, really. For an angel, at least. But they will not hear us. Not from upstairs, not from anywhere. So stop. It's irritating me."

Charms? Angels? It's more than my mind can take in.

"But *why are you here*?" The question escapes in spite of me.

He purses his full lips into a line. "I have been watching you, chthonus. I require your help."

What could I possibly have to offer such a creature? And that word again. *Chthonus.* It unsettles old things I pushed aside long ago. Reminds me of everything I wish to forget.

"Adem." I say it as loud as I dare.

"What?"

"My name. It's Adem."

The angel observes me with sharp eyes, catches every twitch of my face. Every muscle in me tenses. I try to stop the twitches, not to let my edginess show.

"A chthonus with a name. How original," he says. "But then, I knew you were exceptionally well crafted or I would not be here. And it's even clearer close up. You radiate like a furnace, such great magic compounding inside you for so many years. I can feel it from across the cellar."

He stretches his hand out to me like he is warming his fingers.

"Which, of course, is why I am here."

"I am nothing."

He stares at me blankly. "Nothing? Do you know what a chthonus *is*?"

I know. More from the Texts than my own experience, but I know what I am. "Mud."

He shrugs, light and shadow dance over his shoulders. "Mud. Dirt. Dust. Whatever debris men can find. But it's more than the materials. Men create chthonuses to do the work they can't, or won't. For their strength and durability. For their mindless obedience. But men were not meant to create in the first place—that is for the gods alone. Man's magic is stolen from angels, and they do not wield it well. Very few men have succeeded in creating a chthonus, and even then, the process is precarious and unpredictable. Most chthonuss who succeed are grotesque, miserable, broken things."

His words pile up, confirming what I've always felt. "Like me."

He frowns. "Not like you. That's what I'm saying. You are a masterpiece compared to most. You may be hardly more than a live puppet, but most chthonuss are much less."

If I'm among the better ones, the others truly are doomed.

"But enough of this," Kythiel presses. "There is much to say and little time. The reason I have broken through the Host to find you in this temple is this: Chthonus, there is a way for you to be free."

The words seep deep into my chest.

Free.

The world around me fades and I drop into a haze of disbelief.

"Do you understand me, chthonus? I can free you." Kythiel's voice is laced with impatience. It's too much, too good to be true.

"How?"

"I can give it to you. But first you must help me."

"Help you?" What could I possibly have for so perfect a creature?

But...to be free.

"How?"

His lip quivers at the corner.

"For you to understand, I must start at the Beginning. Listen. As it reads in the Texts, in the Beginning—Terath's true Beginning, when man was new—angels had open passage between the Host and Terath. There was no need for a divide between the realms back then. The First Creatures walked side by side with man."

"I know about the Beginning," I say. I've read the tired Text pages over and over and over. Everyone knew them, once. The humans looked after the realm; the angels were Theia's messengers to them, teaching Her Order. The Beginning was beautiful, perfect. Until the men and First Creatures broke the Three's will.

Kythiel scoffs. "From what? The Texts? The Three did not share everything with men. To know all, you had to be there."

But what more could there be? The Texts are everything. "What do you mean?"

Kythiel leans toward me. "The Texts only tell what the Gods wanted to share with men. But for the First Creatures, it was different. When the Three created men, we did not understand. They already had us. The humans did not have our beauty, nor our understanding. But, their great heart and individuality soon won us over."

He pauses, his gaze drops to the ground for a moment.

"One of the first women was Rona. She was different from the others—truly different, not in the trivial ways the others were. Theia singled her out with a special gift: unlike most humans, who needed the angels to reach Theia, Rona knew the Goddess's will and judgment in her dreams. She was beautiful in every way."

He spreads out his hand as he speaks and light bursts from his palm, twisting, and whirling. A face starts to take form, a full bust. Striking wide-set cheekbones, full, proud lips. Her eyes are rich, dark, and deep, matching the dark hair that runs past her shoulders and down her back.

Beautiful. She truly was.

"I was Theia's counselor in the village where Rona lived. Her gift became evident, and we spent endless hours walking and discussing Theia's Order. Even living at Theia's side, I had never understood some of Her mysteries the way Rona could. Over time, I came to love her deeply, and she loved me."

He pauses to take in her image before he continues.

I cut in, my question refusing to stay in me any longer. "But what does this have to do with me?"

He jumps and closes his hand into a fist. Rona's face disappears. He looks back to me.

"Patience. I am getting there." He sighs. "Other angels also came to care more deeply for certain humans. It was impossible not to, they were all so different. Some of them started to couple with human mates. Theia was furious at this and forbade the angels to continue. She placed them in different communities far from the ones they loved. The angels were heartbroken. With Her Will planted in our hearts, we angels had no choice but to obey."

"But humans, with their free will, were not so easily stopped from seeking out the angels they called their own, and the angels' hearts were helpless against such powerful feeling. Their love for their humans set a wedge between the angels and Theia. As the wedge grew, some of them began to find they could choose for themselves, and were no longer bound to Theia's Will as strongly. She was furious at her angels' straying."

"Is that why She called you back?" I find myself absorbed in his story, in spite of myself. The Texts don't give a reason.

"Yes."

A tear waits to drop at the corner of his eye. "She called us back to the Host and set barriers between the realms so we could never return. But there were some angels so consumed with their love they could choose their own will, and they resisted. They fought back."

Barriers. Suddenly the red-haired woman is at the front of my mind. And the boy, too. So close, every day, just outside my window. Yet I could never break free and be one of them.

But that's not important right now. I pull myself back to the moment.

"The First Realm War."

The Texts warn against straying from the Three, tell stories of the terrors of the First War. But they don't speak of this, of why the First Creatures fought against them.

"Yes," he says. "When we were called back, my heart ached for Rona so strongly I was sure part of it had broken off and stayed with her. She also suffered greatly, and I watched her from the Host with no way to comfort her. But I did not fight. I was too bound to Theia to fight against Her, and too consumed in being separated from Rona for anything else."

He pauses. I search my mind for something to say, but the silence is heavy between us. Thankfully, he starts again.

"We all watched over our beloveds from the Host. Angels' hearts are made to be constant and unchanging. The angels loved their human mates until their dying day and will continue to on until forever. But men," Kythiel's tone deepens into a growl, darkness clouds his eyes. "Men move on quickly. They mourned losing their angel lovers at first, but eventually they forgot them and found comfort elsewhere. Many despaired and lost their connection to Theia altogether, wandering away to Terath or the Underworld and never finding their way back."

I've seen it myself, how quickly men can change. How quickly they forget old ways, old friends, wars, even the Gods.

"But my Rona did not forget me. She cried out to me in her prayers, and I heard her pain. She left for days, wandering, trying to find a way into the Host, but Theia had left no gate unsealed."

Kythiel's velvety voice rings with pride.

"It hurt me to see her in such suffering. Each day was worse than the one before, and finally, my desperation helped me discover I could reach her in her dreams the way Theia did. The first time I found her in her sleep, we were filled with ecstasy. But she was unhappy in her life, and we longed for each other every moment she was awake and we were apart. Our love grew so deep that the hours she was awake and I could not be with her, I felt half of myself was missing."

His eyes hollow with desperation. I instinctively step away, resisting their pull. Why is he telling me all this?

"I came to hate my ties to Theia, for while others slipped away to Terath, they bound me to the Host. But at least my Rona was loyal. Some humans were happy to see their angels again, but others had already forgotten, or would not leave their new partners, or were too old to start over again by the time their angels broke free of Theia's hold. When this happened, the angels fell into despair. And in their despair, they lost their way and were unable to return to the Host. They were trapped in Terath, alone and heartbroken."

Lost in Terath? Locked out of their home? It was no wonder some of the First Creatures turned away from the Gods.

"The angels felt all the bitterness of this cruel trick, and they rebelled. They sought other human companions to ease their loneliness. They wandered the land and led humans away from the Three with promises of other great ones, usually themselves. Because they could harness magic, which humans do not understand, they had no trouble gaining followers. Some even taught magic to their human followers. They became free and wild and no longer cared about the Three's Order."

Kythiel's eyes are large and tense. He stares past me a moment, then drops his gaze to the ground.

"I spent all the time I could in Rona's dreams, and the rest of it thinking of her, content with what I had for myself. So much so I didn't see how Rona was slipping away, the toll this double life was taking on her. Not until it was too late. She grew weary, then strained, then desperate. I realized after, she had become trapped in her own mind. Finally, she could bear it no longer. She shut herself off from the Host and, unable to reconcile her worlds waking and asleep, she killed herself."

Kythiel's voice wavers and he bows his head, rubs his eye with his palm. The abrupt end of his story leaves a dead weight through the empty cellar.

He wants my help? With this?

"This all passed long ago. There is nothing I can do for you."

"No! You're wrong!" The marble figure steps toward me, comes forward until his face is inches from mine. His perfect features crinkle into deep sadness, his eyes churn wild. "Bring her back to me."

My hope for freedom snuffs out. I step away from the great creature, my head shaking slowly side to side.

"You would need your Goddess for that."

His great inky wings ruffle. "Theia does not disrupt the Order she set," he scoffs. "She is not a Goddess of mercy, but of rules."

I take another step back. A pit twists in my stomach. "This is not my quest. Go and find her yourself."

Kythiel's fist slams into the wall and rattles the temple's foundation. I flinch, remembering the humans just above. Are they still there? I try to listen for signs of them. But Kythiel roars at me.

"Don't you think I've tried? Do you think I would be here if there was any other way? I have been searching for a way to bring my Rona back ever since she left me. Centuries. But I am as bound to Theia as you are to that box. Even coming here to you was a struggle. And even if I could break that bond, even then—angels are all soul. Souls cannot free themselves of the Underworld. It has to be you. You're a chthonus, man-made, nothing more than mud. You have no soul. You can enter the Underworld and bring her back from it."

The Underworld. He wants me to break into the Underworld. Steal a soul back. He must be mad. "Find another chthonus."

"There are no others like you," his words are rushed and tight. "I watched you for almost a century before I managed to break free tonight. In all that time there has been nothing close to what you are. Oh sure, men have had the hubris to attempt to create life like a god before, but none held the magical power or skill that your maker did. It has to be you. You're my only hope."

His wild eyes empty to a dire hollow. I know this look. I see it often. When the Silencers take a child from a mother, a wife from husband. Humans do wild, desperate things when they look like this.

It only lasts a moment. He straightens up, smooths out his face.

"I'm your only hope too, chthonus. Has anyone else come to you offering freedom?"

No. In all my centuries, they only came to destroy me, to take the box. It's been my whole life. All I've known. Protecting it. Trying to destroy it. Now here it is, a way out. Dropped from the sky right into my hand.

But the price. It is more than I am capable of. I don't know if it is even possible. I study the pain etched across his face. Could he bear it if I failed?

"I don't know—"

He abruptly collapses into a gleaming heap at my feet, dark wings sprawled at his sides.

"What is it you want? I will get it for you. Anything, anything you ask. Just please save my Rona. Bring her back to me."

What do I want?

It's an easy question. All I want, all I've ever wanted, is for the hunt to end. For the killing to stop. To be free of the box.

To be free to live.

And here it is.

For the first time, in all those dark years, I see beyond the box, beyond my small prison. And all I find there is more darkness. More empty corners. More nothing. I could never fit among the humans. Not like this. That would take more than freedom.

"I want to be human."

I jump at the sound of my own voice. I didn't mean to say it aloud. But it throws from me loud, angry, packed with endless years of splintered emptiness.

Kythiel's head snaps up to me.

"What?"

Now that I have said it, I know it's true. This ache has festered in me all these years. This is what I want.

No, what I need.

"Make me human."

Kythiel shakes his head. "That requires a soul," he says.

"Then I will help you for a soul."

Silence. It drags on like a stick in setting mud.

Finally Kythiel speaks, his lip quivering. "I cannot give you that. Souls come from the Three, and the Three alone."

No.

"This is my price."

"You do not want a soul. A soul is pain. A soul is weakness. A soul is death."

A soul is life.

"You said anything. A soul. Make me human."

The need for it burns through me like a hollow tree set on fire from within. I cannot, I *cannot* go on without it. Now that the idea has caught within me, nothing can extinguish it.

The angel droops. His wings, his shoulders, his head.

"I can't give you that."

Silence buzzes between us. Despair pours out of his eyes. My hope hardens and turns to anger.

"Then I must go back." I turn to the stairs, resigned.

"Wait!"

His exclamation is wet, almost a sob.

The air hangs heavy. Kythiel paces the cellar, rubbing his neck, his mouth half forming the words as he mumbles to himself, wrestling, weighing.

I use all my bulk to become immovable. A soul. Nothing else.

Nothing else can give me what the humans have. The love, the passion that fills their short lives so fully, fuller than all I could muster from my hundreds. The connection to each other.

To be free of the box and have nothing to go to, it would be even worse than now. It would be nothing. But a soul...to be one of them...

I would try, risk anything for this.

Kythiel's pace slows as he turns toward me yet again. He stops an arm's reach from me.

"You will have it. After you retrieve Rona."

His words are like magic. Something in me lightens until I feel I am floating. Under it, something nags at my gut—something not quite right. Something too easy. But in my chest, there's a burning, craving hole where my soul will go. I shove the caution away into the shadows, take a deep breath, and let the tension break away into the air. A soul. My very own. Just thinking of it loosens my shoulders and sends tingles up my neck, like I am floating.

"Then we are settled? I must go," Kythiel says. And he begins to turn away with finality.

"Wait!"

A million doubts cloud my mind, a tangle of eagerness and fear. He turns back to me halfway, watching me with defeated disinterest.

So many questions. I pull one out as quickly as I can the one closest to the surface. "How do I get to the Underworld?"

"Walk to the sea. Row out on the water until the sky touches the waves on all sides. Swim West. It will be easiest to break through on the new moon," he says. "When you have her back on Terath, I will come to you."

He begins to turn away, and then looks back to me. "And hear me—Trust no one and nothing. The realm of the Underworld is strange and inconstant.

Abazel is ruthless and deceptive. He will say anything to confuse, hurt, and hold you there, anything to prevent you from bringing her back to me. Do not believe his lies. Many have been lost to him."

Abazel, the demon king. The name turns my stomach. The myths of his wrath, his destruction in the Realm Wars, were once the stories that kept children up at night. The Texts say he started it all. That he is the root of the brokenness that still has the realm in chaos.

Kythiel releases a soft sigh, his pearly, brooding forehead tightening into troubled creases.

"You are my only hope, chthonus. Don't fail me."

Then he turns and walks away, his glow bursting into blinding light. And then he is gone, and I am alone again in the temple cellar.

Chapter 2
Sneak Peek: Mud, Chronicles of the Third Realm War #1

Some books include the Also By information on the same page as the author bio, but many have a separate page dedicated to sharing more works by the same author or publishing house that the reader might be interested. This page can be a very powerful marketing tool.

The text on this page is typically center aligned.

Chapter 3
Sneak Peek: Mud, Chronicles of the Third Realm War #3

Some books include the Also By information on the same page as the author bio, but many have a separate page dedicated to sharing more works by the same author or publishing house that the reader might be interested. This page can be a very powerful marketing tool.

The text on this page is typically center aligned.

About the author

E. J. Wenstrom believes in complicated heroes, horrifying monsters, purple hair dye and standing to the right on escalators so the left side can walk. She writes dark speculative fiction for adults and teens, including Departures and the Royal Palm Literary Awards' Book of the Year, Mud, the first novel in her Chronicles of the Third Realm War series. When she isn't writing fiction, E. J. Wenstrom has written for BookRiot, DIY MFA, The Hot Sheet, and The Write Life, and co-hosts the and podcasts.

Get bonus content and sneak peeks when you join E.J.'s newsletter at EJW enstrom.com

You can also find her on TikTok, Instagram, Threads and Facebook as @EJWenstrom.

Acknowledgements

Christopher, you already know, but it bears repeating. Thank you for supporting me in this pursuit, which sometimes makes me a bit nutty and perhaps a little challenging to be around. Without your support to carve out the time, space, and mental energy to pour myself into this ridiculous endeavor every day, I would be nowhere.

Reba and Sammy: You instilled in me from a very early age that I am in charge, I am awesome, and I am right. Thanks for that. And sorry. Mom and Dad: The older I get, the more I realize that maybe you were right.

To all those crazy pro-level writers out there who are able to consistently crank out 2,000+ words a day: I have lived this now, and it was terrifying. So much respect.

And for my writer friends who, like me, are just trying to write their hearts out every day and hope it finds some readers ... you inspire me every time I talk to you. Thank you for giving me the several-times-over hand up that I needed to get here.